HOWLER

UNTAMED SONS MC MANCHESTER CHAPTER

JESSICA AMES

MANCHESTER CHAPTER
HOWLER
UNTAMED SONS MC BOOK ONE

USA TODAY BESTSELLING AUTHOR
JESSICA AMES

Copyright © 2021 by Jessica Ames

www.jessicaamesauthor.com

Howler is a work of fiction. Names, places, characters, and incidents are a product of the author's imagination and are fictitious. Any resemblance to actual persons living or dead, events, or establishments is solely coincidental.

Editing by Sheri Mireles

Proofreading by Gem's Precise Proofreads

Cover Model: Logan Blackthorn

Photographer: Wander Aguiar

Alpha/Beta readers: Lynne Garlick, Clara Martinez Turco, Allisyn Pentleton, Pat Labrie, Jayne Rushton

Please note: this book contains material aimed at an adult audience, including sex, violence, and bad language.

All rights reserved. Except as permitted under Copyright Act 1911 and the Copyright Act 1988, no part of this publication may be reproduced, distributed, or transmitted in any form or by any means, or stored in a database or retrieval system, without the prior express written consent of the author.

This book is covered under the United Kingdom's Copyright Laws. For more information visit: www.gov.uk/copyright/overview

AUTHOR'S NOTE

This book contains upsetting themes. For a full list of these themes visit:

https://www.jessicaamesauthor.com/jessicaamestwcw

This book is set in the United Kingdom. Some spellings may differ.

CHAPTER 1
PIA

Sometimes, I dream of killing everyone.

It's not a passing thought, either. Given the chance, I would do it.

This is who they made me. They created this new monster before them. Before I was taken by the Road Jesters MC, I was a different woman.

Now…

I would burn the clubhouse to the ground and not give a passing care to anyone who perished in the flames. I would destroy every brother, every club whore, and every old lady in this building.

And I would dance on each of their graves, smiling and laughing as I did.

There isn't enough hate for what I feel for these people.

"That's it, baby." Wrecker's disgusting voice pulls me back to the reality I am trying so desperately to escape.

There is no way out.

This is my life. They own me.

Body.

Soul.

But never heart. That piece of me, I will never give over to them. As long as I'm breathing, I'll always keep that. They want to break me, and have tried many times, but they can't. You can't break what's already broken, and I was damaged long before I was sold to this club.

"Fuck." Wrecker rolls his hips, pushing deeper into my pussy. I try to block out what he's doing, ignoring the pain as he forces himself into me.

"Take me deeper, Pia."

I wish he would keep his mouth shut. His talk makes my stomach roll. It's not sexy. It just reminds me that I have no control over my life.

I don't fight. I haven't for a long time now. Fighting only makes him hurt me more, but internally I'm screaming at him to get fucked. He has no idea how many times I've fantasised about slitting his throat while he sleeps after he's finished with me.

"Who owns this pussy?" he demands as he thrusts harder into me. My insides protest at his roughness.

I don't answer. It's the only defiance I have left. Wrecker isn't a man to be ignored. He grabs my chin, his fingers bruising my skin as he forces me to meet his gaze. "Who?" he hisses, spittle collecting at the corners of his mouth as his eyes flame with anger.

I grit my teeth.

He hits me across the face hard enough to rattle my

skull. "It's been almost three months since I took ownership of you and you're still as defiant as ever."

He thinks it's a game I play with him, denying him. It's not. I loathe him. I will always despise everything he and his stupid club stand for.

You don't own me.

I want to snarl out the words, but I know better. Wrecker has ways of hurting me that are medieval in nature.

At first I'd thought I would be found.

People who are loved don't just disappear.

And I am loved, despite what Wrecker tries to make me believe.

My mum would fight for me. I know she would. Growing up, it was just the two of us. I never knew who my father was. She wouldn't tell me, and I never cared enough to press. If he wanted to be there he would.

In the beginning, I thought she would save me, as she has many times in my life.

But this is different. This is bigger than her.

The Jesters are known in the area, and not for good reasons. They're dangerous men. Even if Mum knows where I am, she can hardly walk into the clubhouse and demand me back.

And that's if she even knows where to find me.

The way Wrecker took me means there were few clues left behind.

He drives into me so hard it splinters my thoughts. I gasp, my back arching as I try to escape what he's doing to me.

Pain tears through my pussy, making tears stand in my eyes. I won't let them fall. I'll never give him the satisfaction of seeing me cry. Instead, I focus on trying to remain relaxed.

He grabs my throat, cutting my air supply off as he pounds me into the mattress. I can't breathe, but I force myself to remain calm. Wrecker won't go so far as to kill me. He likes playing with me too much to give me up, but he'll push me to the edge and watch me teeter on it.

I meet his stare as he continues to stroke in and out of me and smirks at the hatred that crosses my face. He knows I despise him. He isn't stupid or blind. I wear my emotions clearly.

Wrecker releases his hold on my throat and I suck in air as his hips jerk and he spills inside me, grunting his pleasure. The mattress beneath me feels hard, the springs digging into my spine as he pushes me down while his body twitches with his orgasm.

Nausea rolls over me as he rolls his hips, slowing his thrusts. I have the implant so I don't worry about pregnancy, but I do worry about diseases. I have no idea how many women he's stuck his pencil dick into. The club bunnies with the Road Jesters are used by every brother in this club, swapping and sharing in one big fucking orgy, though most brothers do wrap it up. No one wants to knock a bunny up.

Wrecker pulls out of me after a moment, bringing my mind back to the room. I feel exposed, dirty, crawling in the filth he has covered me in. I don't move, keeping my hands fisted at my sides. The urge to slam one into his smug face is overwhelming, but I know better. I don't do anything but watch as he clambers off the bed. His softening dick taunts me as he straightens. I would cut if off in a heartbeat and feed it to him.

If they let me have sharp objects.

One of the other brothers, Griller, learnt the hard way about letting me within reach of anything that could be used as a weapon. That incident earned me a beating that put me in bed for a fortnight.

I watch as Wrecker grabs his t-shirt and pulls it over his head. "You know, it wouldn't kill you to do a little fucking work. You just lie there like a corpse. It's fucking annoying."

I swallow the bile that is climbing up my throat. "Because I don't want you near me." My words are barbed and dangerous. He's battered me for less, but I can't control my mouth tonight. I'm tired of always taking his shit.

I brace for his attack.

It doesn't come. He's too busy dressing and I guess he's in a good mood after getting off. "You should be grateful I let you stay fucking breathing, all things considered."

"How long are you going to hold me accountable for something I didn't do?" I demand, slowly sitting up. I don't bother reaching for the sheets or blankets on the bed to cover myself with. It wouldn't matter anyway. I lost that piece of my dignity a long time ago.

"For as long as I want." He has his jeans on now and grabs his kutte off the back of the chair where he'd hung it before climbing on top of me. He shows that piece of leather more care than he's ever shown me.

"How long?" I press.

It's foolish to rile him, but I need to know when this nightmare will end—if it ever will. Hope is a dangerous weapon, but it's also all I have left to cling to.

Wrecker moves to the edge of the bed and stands over me. He's huge, with dark hair and a thick thatch of beard that covers his jaw. His blue eyes are dead. There's no soul in them. It scares me looking into them, because I don't see any humanity. I have no doubt my end will come at the hands of this man, though I no longer fear dying. It's too exhausting to live in fear constantly, so I put that terror into a box in the back of my mind and ignore it.

"I own every part of you, Pia. You're mine until I decide otherwise." His fingers hook into my hair, tugging my head back so far I feel my neck might snap. He presses his mouth against mine, his kiss bruising and possessive. My split lip, a previous injury, stings. I don't fight him, but I don't reciprocate, either. I'll never respond to the shit he does to me.

His disgusting tongue slides into my mouth, pressing against mine. It's a violation that makes me want to hurl. I can't remember the last time I kissed someone I loved.

Max.

His name drifts across my mind and I hate that I give him room in my thoughts.

He was the man I once loved.

He was the man who held my heart in his palm.

In the end he'd been the one to damn me.

If he'd cared, he would never have left me to this fate. This isn't something I'd wish upon my worst enemy.

"I shouldn't have to pay for his mistakes," I say quietly when he releases my mouth.

Wrecker's fingers tighten in my hair. "Who else can? Max isn't around to make amends."

The injustice of it burns my throat like embers. "Did you even look for him?" I'm not in a position to make demands, but righteous anger tears through me.

"Why would I bother when I have what I want here? You are never leaving my side, Pia. I will kill you before I allow you your freedom."

His words had frightened me when he first brought me to the clubhouse. Now, they leave me feeling hollowed out. I have no escape. The Jesters clubhouse is a fortress. There's no way out without a brother and there's not a single man inside this building that would risk Wrecker's wrath by helping me to escape. None of the women, either. I tried in the beginning to gain the trust of people who could help me escape, only to feel the bitter sting of betrayal. These people are loyal to their president.

Wrecker didn't gain that through respect, but fear.

And they have good reason to be scared of him. I've seen Wrecker's handiwork for myself. I know how lethal he is.

He releases me and shoves me with enough force to momentarily wind me. "Get cleaned up."

I track him as he goes to the door and steps out of the room, leaving me alone. It feels too small, too quiet, the walls closing in. I swallow hard, trying to keep my equilibrium. I want to break down, but I can't. Not here. I can never show any weakness—nothing that can be used against me.

Slowly, I swing my legs out of the bed and stand.

My legs wobble for a moment before I'm able to walk into the en suite bathroom. On autopilot, I shower, removing all traces of him from my body, washing away the blood and cum. As much as I scrub, I never feel clean. If I survive this, if I reclaim my life back, I have no idea how I'm supposed to go back to my normal life, and pretend this never happened. Pretend my ex-husband didn't stab me in the back to save his own skin.

Drying myself, I ignore my reflection in the mirror over the sink. I don't want to see my lank blonde hair, the bruises, and my healing split lip. I don't want to see how emaciated I look. I know my hip bones protrude. My ribs, too. I was always curvy before. It was one of the things Max loved about me.

I return to the bedroom and pull on the thin tee I'm permitted to wear. No underwear. Wrecker likes me accessible. Then I crawl back onto the filthy mattress, curling into a ball. I'm tired. I have to keep fighting, but every time he rapes me he chips away another piece of me that I don't know how to reclaim. I'm empty inside.

A shell.

I don't know how much more I can take of this.

I need a miracle and I gave up on those a long time ago.

CHAPTER 2
HOWLER

The Manchester chapter of the Untamed Sons sits in a building in the Ancoats area, north of the city centre. It's not as big as our mother chapter in London, but it's mine and I'll fucking defend it to my last breath. I was nearly thirty when Ravage, our national and London president, gave me the keys to the city. I didn't expect the war I had to fight to keep what was mine. I'd thought the Sons name would open doors. It didn't. No one in Manchester gave a fuck about the London chapter. They didn't have the reach to defend a city two hundred miles away, which left me fighting for every scrap of land we had.

It wasn't easy. Manchester has a large gang presence, one I've spent years cleaning out.

It took time.

It took lives.

It spilt blood.

But the Sons own the fucking city now.

All of our enemies are gone, crushed into the dirt or turned into supporters and allies. Even the fucking Wood syndicate. They were a huge problem for us, until they took on another London syndicate. Now, they're a fucking footnote.

I peer around the common room, taking in the shabby furniture, the sofa that's seen better days, and the battered pool table that's missing some of the balls.

It stinks of weed and stale booze, but this is home.

My legacy.

One day I hope my kids will wear my club patch with pride.

A group of club bunnies walk past in barely-there denim shorts and tops that show more skin than material. I watch as Brewer, my treasurer, snags Lissa around the waist and pulls her against him.

I can't begrudge him this shit. Brew and all my brothers in arms have been at my side through the hell of the past few years. Strong and steadfast, they are men who have stood by me through the worse battles we've faced. I trust each and every one of them with my life.

That's what this club means to us.

Brotherhood.

Loyalty.

Honour.

Life.

The life we lead isn't for everyone. There's a certain personality that fits in a motorcycle club, particularly one that lives outside of the law like the Sons. Not everyone has the stones for it, and over the years I've seen a shit ton of prospects flame out. Those who dedicate themselves and make it through the recruitment process become closer than blood.

"There ain't enough eye bleach for the shit that goes on in this room." Blackjack, my vice president, pulls out the stool opposite where I'm sitting and parks his arse on it, his pint glass sliding onto the table top. Like all of the brothers in my club, Blackjack is massive. He was a soldier in a former life and is fucking lethal with a knife. Never seen a man play cards like he does either, which is how he earned his road name. I've lost more than my share of money to the fucker.

"Don't look," I tell him, reaching for my bottle and taking a long swig of it.

His kutte, like mine, is worn around the neck and armholes. We've both had our colours on our back for a long while. The patches may have changed from London to Manchester, but the vest never did. I've been wearing the same piece of leather since I first took my prospect patch when I was eighteen. It's moulded to me like a second skin.

"Everything in place for tomorrow?" I ask.

Blackjack and Socket, my secretary, are supposed to be heading down to our Birmingham chapter to collect some weapons that were shipped over from the States. Omen, the Tennessee chapter president, keeps us well-stocked. Guns are brought into London and then moved around to our UK chapters where they are needed. In the past, we were going through a shit ton of stock, but things have been a lot calmer lately.

I can't say I don't enjoy this pace.

As much as I thrive on the fight, it's tiring constantly being on defence.

"Yeah, we're heading out about ten am. I spoke to Grub this morning and everything is ready." Grub is Birmingham's VP and a fucking good brother. He has come to help us numerous times over the past years. Bleed one Son, you bleed us all. Grub firmly believes that shit.

So do I.

My attention is snared as the common room doors are flung open and a dark-haired woman steps inside. Her gaze frantically moves around the room. She is out of place, at odds with the bitches fucking and sucking their way around the room. If I had to guess, I would put her in her late forties, but she looks younger. If it weren't for the lines around her eyes, lines that tell me she either laughed a lot or frowned too much, I would have placed her in her thirties. She is wearing a pair of jeans and a sweater that falls off one shoulder. She is too dressed to be a bunny. Too dressed to a be hangaround, too. She fucking sticks out like a beacon.

I take her in with a sweeping glance, seeing all of that in a split second and instantly going on guard. Her eyes stop on Socket, who has a blonde head between his legs. Trina is sucking his cock.

I come to my feet, expecting trouble. Socket doesn't have an old lady—that I know about. I don't exactly keep track of that shit, but this bitch looks like she means fucking business. I don't plan on sitting around while some crazy cunt shanks a brother in front of me. We lost Crow a few years back and that shit still stings.

Socket takes a moment longer than I do to see the woman, and when he does he does a double-take. I push out from behind the table, making it teeter as I do, and I feel Blackjack at my heels as I move towards the unfolding trouble.

Socket pushes Trina away, quickly tucking his cock back into his jeans as he gets up from the sofa he was sprawled on. The woman covers her eyes, as if she's offended by what she's seeing.

"The fuck are you doing here, Valentina?" he hisses.

"I need your help."

"Problem?" I ask. The bitch doesn't seem armed, but that doesn't mean she isn't dangerous. I'm not taking a chance.

Socket's whole demeanour changes. My brother runs a hand over his grey-streaked black beard. He's one of the oldest of my club officers at forty-five, but the man is fucking dangerous. He is a genius with electrical shit; there's nothing he can't wire. That includes the shit we need for our grow house that brings in a shit ton of revenue every month. Marijuana has become trendy among the student population in Manchester in recent years and as the number of students grows, the more we sell.

"No, she's just leaving." Socket grabs her arm, tugging her towards the door.

The woman, Valentina, tears out of his grip. He snags

her again, trying to get her out of the common room. "Pia's in trouble, Gavin."

Socket stops. "The fuck are you talking about?"

He releases her and she brushes her fingers through her hair as she tries to control herself.

"She disappeared. A few months ago. The police were useless. When I found out where she was, they wouldn't go and get her out."

"Valentina, where the fuck is my daughter?"

His daughter?

I had no idea Socket had a kid. He's never fucking mentioned her. Not in all the years he's been with the club. I don't feel betrayed by his omission, but I wish he would have told me about his kid. I wouldn't have judged.

Valentina swallows hard and meets his eyes. "The Road Jesters took her."

Socket jolts at her words. Jesters are another MC who operate in the southwest of the city. They've never tried to encroach on our patch so we've left them the fuck alone, but if these cunts have Socket's kid, we'll face them.

"You stay here. I'll get her back."

He starts to move, and I speak up. "Socket. Hold the fuck on. You aren't going alone, but I need some explanation here."

Socket lets out a breath. I can see how affected he is by this shit. His body is wired tight, the cords in his neck standing to attention. "Valentina and I have a daughter together. She's twenty-six."

"You never mentioned her, brother," Blackjack says.

"I got locked up not long after she was born. By the

time I got out, she was fifteen. I didn't think it was fair to just drop into her life. I didn't want her caught up in my shit, either. Fuck knows my life isn't exactly without complications. Didn't want to put that on my kid."

I already knew he was locked up shortly after his nineteenth birthday and didn't get out until he was thirty-four. He found the club in the years after. He must have got Valentina pregnant just before he went inside.

"Not asking for help," Socket says. "This is my shit. I'll fix it."

"Ain't letting you go alone," I repeat.

"Prez, this isn't your fight."

"Brother, we ride as one or we don't ride. She's family. Your family. That makes her club. We'll get her back."

Gratitude washes over his face and he clamps a hand on my shoulder. "Thanks, Howler."

"Thank me when she's home." I turn to Valentina. "Why do you think the Jesters have her?"

"Her husband was mixed up with them. I hired a private investigator to find her when the police turned up nothing. He looked into their financials. Every inch of their lives. He found out that Pia was taken to pay some sort of debt Max ran up. I don't understand, Gavin. How is a person taken as a debt payment?"

I'd love to say it was unusual, but some of the less scrupulous gangs have similar rules. My club doesn't deal in skin. Ravage would have my balls on a plate and my kutte off my back if I took some bitch as payment for a debt. Not that I would even contemplate it. We don't have much of a moral compass, but there are definitely lines we don't cross.

Socket pulls Valentina into his arms, pressing her against him. "We'll get her back. I promise."

We will. The Jesters are about to get a lesson in what happens when you cross us.

I call church, and for an hour we discuss our options and how best to attack. Then I mobilise the brothers, organising everyone as we prepare our attack. We need to find out as much as we can about the enemy we're facing. Luckily, I've made it my business to know every club, gang and operation in the city, so I know enough about the Jesters to know how to hit them where it'll hurt.

It takes a few days to get everything into place. Agonising days for Socket and Valentina. They want their daughter back and they don't want to wait. I understand that.

On the evening of the attack, we arm up using guns sent over from our US brothers and then we ride to deliver the Jesters' last day.

CHAPTER 3
PIA

I peer at the broken girl in the mirror above the sink. The bathroom is my only refuge from the men who use me as a sex toy. I hate them for it. I hate Max, as well, but most of all I hate myself for taking this shit.

I want to fight. I try, but Wrecker is stronger. So are his brothers.

I'm helpless and that is the worst part of this. The loss of my control.

I run a finger over the split in my lip. My face is starting to swell, my left eye especially. It'll be black by the morning. I swallow with difficulty. Wrecker put his hands around my throat again. He likes to take me to the edge of passing out before bringing me back. That shit left my legs shaking and barely able to hold my own weight, which is why I'm gripping the basin like it's my lifeline.

"The fuck are you doing in there?" Wrecker's voice slides through the thin wood that keeps some distance between us. It's not enough. If he wanted to he could be in this room in an instant.

"I'll be out in a second," I rasp back. My throat is raw.

I rub it, trying to disperse some of the pain, but it doesn't help. I meet my gaze in the mirror. I hate the look in my eyes. The one that says I've given up. I've resigned myself to this life.

It's too hard to keep fighting.

Wrecker and his boys take what they want from me.

I can't stop them.

I'll never be able to stop them.

I sink onto the edge of the tub and though my tears want to fall, they don't. They have stripped me of even the ability to cry. My life with Max was never good. He wasn't quick with his fists, but there are other ways to tear a person down. Max knew every trick in the book. He spent most of our marriage building me up only to knock me back down when he felt I'd overstepped my place. My mother hated him. That should have been my first red flag. Mum is a great judge of character.

I was blinded.

I loved Max. He was my first. My first relationship. My first everything. I thought we'd be together forever. When he first started breaking me down, I didn't understand it. I didn't recognise it, either. He chipped away at me piece by piece. He may have worn a suit but he was more of a crook than the men in leather vests who torment me daily. Max's betrayal was worse. He was supposed to give a shit about me.

In the end all he proved was that he valued his own life over mine.

A fist hammers on the door again. I steel myself and release the breath that feels lodged in my throat.

Then I open the door. Wrecker is standing next to it, his eyes bright. This terrifies me because it means nothing good is coming. It's further compounded by the two men sitting on the edge of the bed. Griller and Boulder.

He's going to let his brothers have me tonight.

Fear climbs up my spine. It's not the first time this has happened and that's what drives my terror. These men are sick bastards.

Wrecker winds his fingers into my hair, pulling me back against his chest as Griller moves towards me, Boulder following on his heel.

"My boys got some stress to work out," Wrecker says in my ear. His free hand, the one not in my hair, goes between my legs, roughly pushing through my slit and inside me. I whimper. He hasn't given me enough time to recover. My insides are raw, my body broken.

I can't do this. Please. I need this to stop. I can't take any more.

I disappear into that part of my brain that protects me from what's about to happen. Boulder drops his jeans and pulls his thick, cock out.

"We're going to fuck you bloody," Boulder sneers.

He presses against me, the head of his cock an undeniable presence.

As he's about to shove inside me a barking sound blasts from beyond the door.

I don't compute what it is immediately, but the brothers do. Wrecker releases me as Boulder drags his jeans up. "We'll be back for you, bitch."

They run from the room as more sounds erupt.

Gun fire.

It's gun fire.

It wouldn't be the first time one of the brothers has gotten shit-faced and let off a few rounds, but the blood-curdling scream that follows makes my heartbeat freeze in my chest and tells me this is an attack. Sticky fear clogs my throat.

I force my brain to calm. I have split seconds to make decisions and I need to think rationally.

There is no way out of this room other than moving back through the clubhouse. The window in my room is boarded up to stop my escape.

Hide.

I drop to my knees at the side of the bed and scramble under it, ignoring how claustrophobic it feels to have the slats of the bed base inches from my head. I tug the covers over the edge so I can't be seen from the door and lay flat against the floor as I try to control my breathing. Voices sound closer, the popping of gun fire louder.

I clamp a hand over my mouth to stop from screaming and close my eyes. I live with a devil, but I know what to expect from Wrecker. It's the unknown I fear.

My thoughts scatter as the door crashes open, bouncing against the plasterwork. I see boots from under the slither of space between the carpet and hanging sheet.

Two sets. I hold my breath, willing them to leave as

gun shots continue to pop in the background. I'm not going to die under a bed after a year of being abused. I'm not.

The boots move closer to the bed. The sheet is lifted and I come face to face with dark brown eyes.

"Got you." My foot is grabbed by the owner of the other pair of boots.

I shriek. I can't help it. It slips out unbidden as I'm dragged from under the bed, my nails clawing at the carpet, trying to seek purchase. I find none. I thrash my bare legs out, trying to unseat my attacker's hold, but he doesn't release me. I scratch, claw, throw my arms out—anything to make it stop, but he is stronger than me.

"Easy, wildcat," a gruff voice orders as I'm forcibly restrained. Brown Eyes has hair the same colour kept shorter on the sides than the top. His accomplice is a redhead with a clean jaw and tattoos running up his neck. Between them they hold down my arms and my ankles.

"Take your fucking hands off me," I yell. Panic starts to move though my veins, pressure building throughout. I've learnt to deal with what Wrecker does to me, but letting new people touch me...

I can't do it.

I try to bring my legs together to cover myself, to hide my private parts from these men, but they don't release me. I do notice their holds are not bruising, exerting enough pressure to keep me immobile but not to hurt me. It doesn't stop me from fighting against them, trying desperately to free myself. I don't know what new game this is, but I'm not playing it.

"The club whores are fucking crazy here," Red Hair mutters. He has a Treasurer patch on his kutte while his friend has Road Captain. As he turns I see the Untamed Sons arched over his back. Manchester curves beneath the insignia of a skull wearing a crown with wings behind it. Both men are officers in another MC.

My blood freezes. I know exactly what MCs do to women like me.

For that reason I should shut my mouth, but I'm tired, hurt, and scared. That makes my tongue loose. "I'm not a club whore," I hiss. Wrecker might treat me like nothing more than that but I refuse to let anyone believe I'm here of my own free will.

"Old lady?" Brown Eyes asks.

"I'm…" I sneer as I think the word. "I was forced to be here."

"By who?"

"Wrecker. Who else?"

The two men exchange glances and something passes between them in that moment, something I can't decipher.

"Pia?"

I freeze. How do these men know my name? I'm too scared to answer, but the redhead speaks. "Your mum sent us to find you."

His words don't hit as he probably expects. I'm not jubilant at the rescue but suspicious. "My mother doesn't hang around biker gangs. Why would she send you?"

Another look passes between them. "It's not our place

to tell you, but we're here to help, sweetheart," Brown Eyes says. "You're safe now."

Safe.

Such a foreign word.

And one I don't believe. How can I possibly be safe with these men? I know bikers. They take what they want without thought of what they do.

I shake my head, stepping back a little and putting some space between us. "I'm not leaving."

"Pia, we have to go. Valentina is waiting for you back at our clubhouse."

I want desperately to hope that is true, but trust isn't something that comes easily anymore. I trusted in the past and ended up here. I'm not doing it again.

"No." I move, putting the bed between us.

"I don't want to hurt you, darlin'," Brown Eyes says, "but we can't stay here. The pigs'll be here soon and we need to be gone before that happens. You either walk out of here with us willingly or you don't, but either way you're coming with us."

CHAPTER 4
HOWLER

The Jesters' clubhouse is nothing like the Sons. It's fucking dirty and looks like a squat. Our clubhouse may be rough around the edges, but I can see the lack of respect for what they have in every table, every chair. The sticky floor beneath my feet tells me their prospects aren't worth shit. This wouldn't stand in my house.

I walk among the Jesters lying face down on the common room floor, their fingers laced behind their heads as my brothers point guns at the back of their heads. One wrong move and we'll be redecorating their clubhouse in blood. Their kuttes stare up at me, the Jesters' insignia on the back of them.

Jokers.

Fitting for their club.

Looking around, I'm a little concerned at what state we're going to find Socket's kid in. It's clear these fuckers don't respect women. I can tell by the state of their bunnies. The women are standing to one side of the bar, clinging to each other, their dark eyes wide. All of them are bruised: a blonde with a purple mark to her jaw, a red head with finger marks on her thighs and arms and another woman, also a redhead, has a split lip. Bunnies aren't respected universally. They are someplace to lose tension, not someone you take home, but they don't deserve to be beaten and hurt. I would lose my shit if I found out one of my brothers laid a finger on one of the girls in our club.

We don't prey on women.

It's one of the few rules I have. I watched my mother take beatings from my piece of shit father on the regular —at least, until I was big enough to defend her. I'll never allow a man to lay a finger on a woman in front of me. I see that shit, someone is getting a beating.

It takes a weak man to hit a woman.

"Put the girls in the van," I say to Blackjack.

"You planning on keeping them?" He arches a brow.

I'm not, but I'll give them something they've lost while under the Jesters—a choice.

"No, but we need to make sure they won't talk to the pigs." I'll offer each of them the choice to stay with my club. If they don't want that, they can go back to their lives.

"The fuck is the meaning of this, Howler?" Griller. The Jesters' vice president. There's no sign of their cunt president, Wrecker, but my boys haven't finished searching the building yet. Griller turns his head slightly, trying to look up at me from his prone position on the floor. "You got a fucking death wish?"

That threat is laughable, considering how easily we stormed his clubhouse and seized control.

"You took someone you shouldn't have," I tell him.

"Didn't take no one," he hisses. "This is a fucking act of war."

Socket moves before I can, my brother grabbing Griller by his hair. "You were at war the moment your shithole club laid hands on my fucking daughter."

Confusion bleeds into his eyes.

"Haven't touched your daughter, Socket. Didn't even know you had one."

"It doesn't matter if you knew or not," he snarls into Griller's face. "You fucking took her and I'm going to gut every member of your fucking piece of shit club for it." Socket releases his hair with a shove before he slams his foot into his side with enough force to leave Griller panting. I watch, not intervening. If my brother wants to take his anger out on this fucker I'm not going to stop him.

Besides, if the Jesters really have Pia, then that's just a taste of what we're going to do to him.

She may not have been under club protection before, but she sure as fuck is now.

"I'm going to burn your fucking club to the ground," Griller threatens on a wheeze. He can try, but his club is small. We have the might of multiple chapters and numerous allied brothers at our back. If I need it, I can pick up the phone and have any one of our UK chapters come to my aid. US and mainland Europe too if I ask.

Their size and lack of threat have been the only reasons we've left them alone. They were far enough from our patch not to be a problem, and not established enough to be a risk. I see now that might have been a fucking mistake.

My attention is snapped from Griller by the sound of shrieking. I turn as Trick and Brew step into the room, holding a woman between them. I know instantly she's Socket's kid. She's got the same dark hair he had before his started greying, and they share the same eyes and nose.

Even beneath the bruises that cover her face I can see the similarities.

I fold my arms, trying to control the crushing feeling in my chest as I take in the split to her lip and the swelling to her cheek. These fuckers have clearly been using her as a punching bag.

My brothers try to keep control as Pia thrashes against them, trying to get free of their hold. They're trying not to hurt her while keeping her from running. The struggle makes the ratty tee she's wearing slide up her body, revealing her cunt. There are bruises on her thighs: ugly purple marks that don't paint a happy fucking picture of what's been happening here.

My jaw grits and magma burns through my gut.

There are many reasons why she might not be wearing underwear, but my mind goes straight to the worst-case scenario.

I swallow bile, my head starting to thump as realisation dawns for Socket, too. His face crumples and his eyes close for a moment as he takes in his daughter.

I've known Socket a long time. My brother was patched in before I had a prospect kutte on my back. I've always looked up to him. I respect him. That's why I made him my secretary when I took the gavel. The despair on his face is enough to make me vow I'm going to destroy the Jesters. They're going to burn for this. All of these fuckers are dead.

"Fuck," he spits as he stares at Pia, as if he can heal each of her injuries with his anger alone.

Pia's gaze darts around my brothers, taking in our kuttes, our club name. Her eyes stop on mine and something stirs inside me. A need I can't explain. A want to heal her and hold her.

She shakes her head.

"Take her to the van," I order. We need to wrap this shit up and get gone before the pigs turn up.

Horror dawns on her face. "No... no. I'm not going with another club. You'll have to kill me first." She hisses the words with venom. I can practically see the claws coming out as she starts to struggle against Trick and Brew again. Considering how petite she is, she's giving the brothers a hell of a fight.

"Quit fucking struggling," Trick mutters.

Pia's eyes dart around the room as she licks her lips. "I'm not letting you take me."

"Let her go," I say.

Trick looks at me like I've lost my mind before he

glances at Brewer, who raises his shoulders and releases his hold. Trick does the same. Pia wrenches away, wrapping her arms around her middle. She's outnumbered and surrounded. I can see why she'd be scared.

Socket tears his kutte off and shoves it at me, then he pulls his hoodie over his head, ruffling his hair as he emerges from it. He steps over to Pia and offers her the garment.

She stares at it as if it's live ammunition before she raises her eyes to his. I don't know what the fuck is going through her head. I can only imagine. She was taken by a club who have clearly treated her worse than a fucking dog. Now she's facing another club. She's bound to be suspicious; outright hostile even.

"Take it," he says when she doesn't move. Socket is one step from losing his shit. That's his kid, half naked and bruised to hell, and she doesn't have the first clue who he is.

Her eyes slide around the room, stopping briefly on me. I see so much mistrust behind those baby blues. So much anger and pain, too. Even if she weren't half naked, the haunted look tells me what she's suffered.

Maybe things we can't fix, even with time and healing.

I clench my fingers into a ball at my side.

"We're not going to hurt you, Pia," Socket says, bringing her attention back to him. "We're here to bring you home."

She laughs at that but there isn't a hint of humour in her words. "And I'm supposed to trust you over the pricks you have lined up on the floor? You're an MC. You're just as bad."

"We aren't like those cunts," Trick says, heat punching his words.

Her frightened eyes turn to Trick. "I don't know that, do I?"

"Put the sweater on," Socket orders. She hesitates before she does as she's told. I hand Socket back his kutte, which he slides back on over his tee. No one moves, a standoff ensuing. She's never going to trust us and we're never going to convince her otherwise. Socket looks like he wants to pull her into his arms, but he doesn't move. "Who did this to you?"

Her throat bobs at the snarl in his words. "Wrecker... Boulder... Griller."

Griller roars, "Fucking lying bitch!"

She steels her spine, lifting her jaw. "I'm not lying though, am I? You know what you did to me, you disgusting prick."

Socket runs a hand over his mouth, his eyes as haunted as his daughter's. He doesn't hesitate. He pulls his piece and puts a bullet in Griller's leg. He'll want to torture the fucker, but the clock is ticking down. The pigs are slow in this city, but they will eventually respond. No doubt some nosey fucking do-gooder has already called the police to report a group of bikers descending on the Jesters' clubhouse.

The Jester screams out, clutching his thigh. It'll burn at first, like liquid fucking magma is flowing into the wound before it starts to ache.

"Which one is Boulder?" Socket demands.

He wants to mete out justice. I get it. Understand it and would want to do it myself. I don't have the luxury of giving him the time he needs to exorcise the demons haunting him—and Pia.

"We don't have time for this," I snarl.

We need to be gone.

Especially considering I don't plan on leaving a single member of this club breathing. Righteous anger burns through me. The need to avenge her wrongs weighs heavily on my shoulders. For some reason I find myself wanting to slay all her demons.

Socket holds a hand up.

"Give me a second, Prez." The pleading quality to his voice is all that makes me hold us off. I fold my arms over my chest and huff out a breath.

Socket steps forwards and tries to make himself seem smaller as he gets into Pia's space. It's an impossible task because he's a big guy with wide shoulders and a thick torso. "Darlin', you have to. We can't stay here."

Her eyes dart between him and my other brothers.

She's not going to back down and the clock is ticking.

"Fuck it," I mutter.

I lower my shoulder and slam it into her belly, flipping her over my shoulder. She screams, but I ignore her voice as I shift her weight to a comfortable position. Socket is glaring at me.

"I could have talked her around," he grinds out.

"Yeah, and we'd all be locked up tonight. Clean this

shit up." I say this last part to Trick and Brew. Both brothers nod, knowing what I mean.

After today the Jesters won't be a problem.

I stride through the building, a thrashing Pia against my shoulder. "Quit struggling," I growl.

"Stop fighting against the man trying to abduct me?" she hisses.

I don't stop walking even as her nails claw at my kutte, trying to seek purchase. "You want to stay in this shit hole club instead?"

"No. I want to go home."

"You don't listen too good, do you? That's where we're fucking taking you."

"Before or after you rape me?"

"Not into unwilling bitches," I tell her.

"I don't believe you."

The cold air hits as I reach the doors to the parking area. I push through it and relish the freshness. That fucking common room stank like shit. How does Wrecker let his men live that undisciplined?

I reach the van and lower her off my shoulder. As soon as her feet touch the ground she tries to run. I grab her by the back of the neck and she freezes like I've tasered her.

"Don't." The broken quality of her voice makes me pause. I'm not stupid. The state we found her in—the bruises, the lack of underwear—I can draw conclusions that the Jesters have used Pia in ways no one should ever be used. That fucking enrages me.

No one deserves to have their choices stripped away.

No one deserves to be used and discarded, either.

"I'm not going to hurt you, Pia."

She shrinks into herself, all sign of fight gone in an instant. "I want to believe you. I really do."

"Give you my word. You have the protection of the Sons."

She doesn't say anything, her gaze shifting to the horizon. I see the demons there. Demons Socket may not be able to exorcise.

"If I let go of you are you going to try and run again?" I can see the lie in her eyes as she shakes her head. "Babe, I'm not chasing you. You run and I'll leave you here with the Jesters."

She licks her bottom lip, her eyes darting over my face.

"You're asking a lot here. Trust isn't easily given and my trust has been broken beyond repair. My experience with motorcycle clubs hasn't been good, so how do I know you're any better than those animals in there?" She gestures towards the clubhouse. "I'm not looking to trade one hell for another with a man whose name I don't even know."

I understand her hesitation. We're not giving her any reason to trust us, and I can't offer her assurances, either, but I try. She's Socket's kid and that means something to me. I release my hold on her and raise my hands, a gesture I hope comes across as non-threatening. She doesn't run. I take that as a win.

"My name's Howler. The Sons is my club. I handpicked most of the men in that building, and the few I didn't I've known long enough to know the type of character they have. I know you don't got no reason to trust or take what I'm saying at face value, but we aren't the enemy."

She mulls this over for a second before she shakes her head.

"You're a motorcycle club. The rules don't apply to you. You take what you want, regardless of the consequences."

"Can't deny that. We take plenty and we don't conform to the shit society tells us we have to, but there are lines we won't cross, too. You've got to have some order, even in fucking chaos, babe. Otherwise all you have is chaos." I glance back at the building. "We're not like those cunts in there. The Jesters are rotten to the core and have been for a long time. Wrecker spread through this club like a poison."

She shivers at his name and I wonder if it was the Jesters' president who hurt her. I wouldn't put it past that cunt to be a raping piece of shit.

Her gaze crawls over my face, confusion and uncertainty, and distrust, too, in her eyes. I can see she wants to believe me, but the doubt lingers.

"Why did you come here?"

"To get you out."

"I know that, but why? I've never set foot in your club. I know nothing about you and yet you're here to save me."

I'm not surprised she has questions. This situation is fucking crazy. I want to give her the answers, but it's not my secret to spill. I don't know how Socket and Valentina plan on telling Pia she has a father she's never met. Twenty-six years is a long time to be in the dark. I also don't know how they will help her reconcile the fact her father is a biker, either, considering her mistrust of us.

I pull out a cigarette from the back pocket of my jeans and light it up. I offer her one and she hesitates for a moment before taking one out of the packet. I light hers first, cupping my hand around the flame as I do, then I light mine. The nicotine relaxes every muscle in my body as it seeps through my system.

"Didn't see Wrecker in that room. He on a run?"

"No, he was there right before you busted in. I wouldn't expect to find him, though. No loyalty in that bastard."

I'd gathered that myself. "I know it's asking a lot, but you put your faith in us and we'll see you safe."

She takes a drag of her cigarette and blows the smoke out before speaking again. "The man who found me said my mother sent you. Is that true?"

I nod. "Valentina is back at the clubhouse waiting for you."

I watch as she mulls this over in her head. "Can I speak to her? On the phone? Just to confirm your story."

I don't blame her distrust. In her mind leather kuttes mean pain, suffering. It would be so much easier if we could just tell her who she really is, but I won't do that to Socket.

I let the cigarette dangle between my lips as I reach into my back pocket and pull my phone free. When I hand it to her, I see the surprise cross her face. She didn't think I would give it to her.

"Don't break my trust and call the pigs."

She tucks her hair behind her ear and dials. I watch as she makes the call.

"Mum?" The sob that wracks her body makes my stomach twist.

I finish my cigarette as she turns away a little, giving me her back as she tries to find some privacy.

If I were a decent man I would move away, give her the space she so desperately craves.

But I'm not.

There isn't a decent bone in my body and never has been.

Socket appears in the doorway, his eyes snapping to mine before coming to rest on his daughter. When he sees she is unharmed his shoulders relax. I wouldn't have hurt her, and he knows that, but I think he was worried she might have run.

Blackjack appears behind him and I give him a lift of my chin, a gesture that speaks more than any words.

Take care of this.

He nods his head and pats Socket on the chest. Grudgingly, my brother moves away, disappearing back into the Jesters' clubhouse to finish what we started. My boys will leave no trace of this shithole club. Not for touching one of our own.

I give my attention back to the dark-haired woman standing next to me. She looks like Socket, though she has a lot of Valentina in her, too. I don't judge my brother for the choices he made, but I don't know how he stayed away from his own child for this length of time. I could never do it.

Pia ends the call and steps back to me. Her cheeks are tear-stained, her eyes red as she hands me back my phone. She doesn't try to run, so whatever Valentina said to her has her trusting us. That'll make things easier.

"Mum confirmed your story. She said she'd explain everything when I get back to your clubhouse." She wraps her arms around her middle, making the hoodie her father handed her lift a little. I keep my eyes locked on hers, resisting the urge to let my gaze trail down to her thighs. She's Socket's kid and she's been through hell.

"Those fuckers will pay for what they've done," I assure her.

Her attention goes to the skyline, her gaze distant, and I know the haunted look in her eyes is going to take a long time to disappear. It may never go. I can imagine what these animals did to her while she was in their hold. How does a person get over something like that? "How? How will you make them pay?"

I pull out another cigarette. "We're going to burn their clubhouse to the ground, with them in it."

If my words shock her she doesn't show it. She doesn't seem disturbed by them, either, which tells me what they did to her was so bad she's okay with them burning.

After what feels like an age, she brings her attention back to me, her eyes flaming. "Good." It's all she says, but it's all she needs to. The weight of that word is enough to convey how she feels about the men who held her captive.

She moves to the back of the van and sits on the bumper, just above the towbar. Her dark hair tumbles across her face, providing a curtain that hides the emotions playing over her. I'm not sure I like it. For some reason, I want to know exactly what she's thinking and how to fix it. Destroying the Jesters will go some way to healing her pain, but I'm not stupid enough to think it'll rectify everything.

In the silence spanning between us gunshots echo out. They aren't frantic, but controlled. One shot after another after another. A single, sharp report each time. My brothers will have stood behind the Jesters on the floor of the common room and put a bullet in the back of each man's head. It was a cleaner death than they deserved, but I've never been one for big fanciful showdowns. I prefer to be clean. In and out, job done. Torture was enjoyable, and my sergeant at arms, Terror, would've had a party with these fuckers, but there is a lot to be said for being efficient and just getting shit done.

My eyes drift towards Pia, who flinches with every gunshot. She grips the edge of the van, her knuckles whitening. I don't move or try to offer her comfort. What can I say? My brothers—including you father—killed the men inside that building in cold blood?

She lifts her head, hugging herself tighter, her brows drawing together. "It's... it's over?"

I wish I could give her that reassurance. I wish I could tell her everything is going to be okay now, but I can't.

"Not until we find Wrecker."

I watch her tongue dart out and wet her bottom lip at his name. I don't miss the flinch either. Yeah, that cunt is dying first.

At the sound of voices I glance up and see my

brothers striding out of the clubhouse. Blackjack is tucking a gun into the back of his jeans while Socket pushes to the front of the group, his gaze locked on his daughter. I see the relief roll through my brother as he takes her in.

"You're still here," he says as he gets closer. His fingers twitch at his sides, making me wonder if he's pushing down the urge to pull her into his arms.

"I didn't have anywhere else to go," she responds, a small smile kicking up the corner of her mouth.

Bent but not broken...

Wrecker undoubtedly tried to tear Pia down, break her piece by piece, but that hasn't happened. She's not broken. She's not destroyed. Hope fills me that she can recover from this trauma, and with her family around her she can find her way again.

I turn as Trick backs out of the clubhouse, a petrol can in his hands. Blackjack lights a match and tosses it on the line of gasoline.

It roars into flames, following the accelerant out through the doors.

"Time to go," I say.

Pia stands and I offer her my hand. She frowns for a moment, then takes it. I help her into the van before my brothers pile in behind me, Brewer and Terror sitting in the front—the latter taking the driver's seat. I sink down against the side wall of the van. Pia sits next to me, drawing her knees to her chest and pulling the large sweatshirt down over them.

Socket sits opposite his daughter, his eyes never

leaving her face as Trick gets in last, pulling the back doors shut behind him.

Without warning, Pia slips her palm over mine. I glance down at her small hand. Fuck, she didn't deserve this shit. No one did. I turn my hand and grasp hers in mine. She squeezes me and for the rest of the drive back she doesn't let go.

CHAPTER 5
PIA

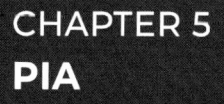

The van rolls and bumps along the busy Manchester streets. I can hear traffic outside the metal cage we're trapped in, everyday noises I missed while in captivity. I don't know how the hell my mother enlisted the help of an MC to get me out of the Jesters clubhouse. I'm not sure I want to know, either. Mum has always been so straight-laced. I can't imagine how she knows these men.

Howler squeezes my hand as the van turns a corner. I don't know what possessed me to grab him, but his touch is the only thing stopping me from losing my mind right now. He shouldn't reassure me. He's a biker. No different from Wrecker and the other bastards he called brothers.

But Howler is different.

So are his men.

They could have hurt me, but so far they haven't done anything but reassure me I'm going to be okay.

I stare at my hand clasped in Howler's and I feel peace

roll through me for the first time in months. I shouldn't let my guard down, but I feel safe. These men are not like the Jesters. When they saw my state of undress they didn't pounce on me. The older guy took his hoodie off and gave it to me.

I didn't understand why, but it soothed some of the voices in my head that told me it was crazy to trust an MC.

I peer around the van, unsure why these men decided to become my white knights, but grateful they did. I don't know how much more I could have taken at the hands of Wrecker and his brothers. I was seconds from breaking. Seconds from falling apart.

My body aches from the torment the Jesters visited upon me, but I'm alive. I'm breathing.

And hopefully I'm safe.

My mother was adamant on the phone I could trust these people, and I trust her with my life.

I can't wait to see her again. To hug her close and have her tell me everything will be okay. I need that more than anything.

Closing my eyes, I let me head drop back against the metal wall behind me and try to centre myself. I'm free. After months of torment, I'm finally free. It doesn't seem real. I thought I would die at the hands of Wrecker. He threatened many times to end my life while he was raping me.

The van stops abruptly, shoving me against Howler. "Sorry," I mutter.

"It's okay," he responds.

Letting go of his hand is the hardest thing I've ever had to do. It feels as if the ground is unsteady beneath me, as if I could fall down at any moment.

Climbing to my feet, my grasp slips from his and I swallow down my fleeting panic. I can do this. I don't need anyone to hold my hand, least of all a biker I just met.

Smoothing down the borrowed hoodie, I make my way to the back of the van and the older guy who gave me the garment is waiting for me. He holds out a hand and helps me down, so I don't have to jump down onto the tarmac. I don't know what his problem is, but he hasn't stopped staring at me since we got into the van. His expression seems to morph between softness and rage. I don't need or want his pity.

He can't fix the broken parts of me that Wrecker and his bastard brothers broke.

I take his hand and let him guide me down on to the ground. The Sons clubhouse is different to the Jesters'. It sits on the edge of the canal, surrounded by red brick buildings. There is evidence of the industrial hub the city used to be, with old mills converted into luxury apartments, the tall chimneys no longer pumping out billowing smoke but decorating the horizon. There are rows of silver and chrome bikes lining the street and a large banner hanging over the doorway of the nearest three-storey building. My eyes scan over the insignia and the 'Untamed Sons' arced over the top. Below, the 'Manchester' sits prominently. The Jesters clubhouse was in the back of an industrial estate, a squat former warehouse with no character. This place oozes interesting.

"Pia…" I turn to older man. "I uh… I need to—"

Before he can say another word a shriek pierces the air. As I turn, I see my mother come barrelling towards me. Her boots are loud in the narrow street, echoing off the high walls that surround the area.

I expect her to throw her arms around me, but as she gets closer she comes to a stuttering halt. It's been only a few months since I saw her last, but the time has changed her subtly. She looks tired, rundown. Her clothes are wrinkled, her eyes smudged beneath with black rings. Guilt crawls through my veins. I did this to her when I married a man who thought nothing about selling me to save his own skin.

Mum's hands fly to her mouth as she takes me in. I know I'm bruised, swollen, my lip cut. I'm suddenly aware of the fact I'm bare beneath the hoodie I was given. Tears brim in my eyes, threatening to fall. I don't want her to see me like this. Don't want her to think I'm weak and fragile.

"Oh, Pia!" The way her voice breaks on my name makes my stomach twist. I hate that I'm causing her distress, that I've made her worry. I never intended for that to happen.

Growing up, it was just me and my mum. She never told me about my father or where he was. I asked questions when I was younger, but the older I got the less I cared. If my father wanted to be in my life, he would be. I've always tried to protect my mother from everything.

That's why I kept it to myself when Max was starting to take money from our joint account. It's why I never said a word when he disappeared into the ether, draining every penny from our bank. It's why the Jesters were able to take me so easily. I never opened up; I never confided in her. If I had, maybe she would have had the police come to the clubhouse straightaway.

Completely in the dark, I have no idea how she found me, but I'm grateful she did.

I let my eyes soften and then I pull her into my arms, ignoring the way my chest aches as she presses against bruised ribs. She clings to me like she never wants to let me go, and I don't want to either. I never thought this day would come. I thought I would be in the hold of the Jesters for the rest of my life—or at least until Wrecker decided to free me.

"I'm so sorry," Mum murmurs into my hair. I don't want to let her go, but eventually I pull free.

"I really want a burger."

Despite everything, Mum laughs. "I'm sure we can get you one, sweetheart."

I feel eyes on me and turn slightly. Howler is watching me, his eyes intense. I can't decide whether he pities me or is angry on my behalf.

He is in his thirties, maybe mid-to-late with dark hair that is spiked up into a messy stack that suits the chaotic feel of the man. His jaw is covered in a thick layer of hair that spans across his top lip as well as his chin, and he has a ring through his nose. A little silver hoop. It's not the only jewellery he wears. He also has tunnels in his ears.

Everything about him screams danger, yet I find myself drawn to him, as if he can offer me all the safety in the world. I let my gaze trail over the tattoos running up his neck to disappear beneath his T-shirt. He is wild, but not in the same way as Wrecker and his men. There is control in Howler, and an iron resolve that I never witnessed in the Jesters' president.

The older brother steps up to us and I see the nervousness move through my mother. Instantly I go on edge. Are these men not to be trusted? Did she make a deal with the devil to get me back?

Even with my injuries I stand between this man and my mother, ready to protect her.

But he doesn't make a move beyond what is already done. He peers down at me, his thick brows coming together.

"You're safe here. You and your mum. No one will touch you." I have no idea why he gives this assurance, but for some reason I believe his words. I don't think he or his club means to harm me. I genuinely think they did rescue me to save me.

Mum comes towards me, wrapping her arm around my shoulders. "Let's get you inside." I want to argue, but I'm aware of my nakedness beneath the hoodie I'm wearing. The street isn't busy; in fact, one end has bollards across the road, stopping the traffic from coming down here from that direction. But there are many windows overlooking the street and I have no idea who might be seeing what state I'm in.

"We need to talk, Valentina," the older man says.

My breath catches in my throat. Does he think I'm going to let him hurt her? I don't care what deal she made for my safe return; it's not going to happen. I can only imagine the devils she got into bed with. I know how these men work, how they think. They would not have rescued me without incentive and I'm terrified to find out what that incentive might have been.

"If you touch her—"

The man holds up a hand, his stance defensive rather than attacking. "I just want to talk."

I twist to glance over my shoulder at my mum, but her eyes have locked on the man in front of me; wide, but there's something else there, too. It's a softness I've only ever seen her direct towards me. Is there something going on between them?

"Gavin, this isn't the best time. Maybe we should—"

He interrupts her before she can finish what she is about to say. "No more waiting. No more putting off what we should have dealt with years ago. It's time."

I have no idea what these cryptic words mean, but I give my mother my full attention, hoping she will explain. Instead, she swallows hard, her throat working as she tries to find the words to rebut him—Gavin. It's not a name I'm familiar with, so I have no idea how she knows him, but it's clear she knows him better than I first thought.

"Please don't do this now."

The desperation in my mother's voice puts me on edge. What doesn't she want him to do?

"Whatever deal she made to get me back, we're not

honouring. I will kill every member of this club if you touch her."

"I'm not your enemy." His eyes seek out my mother again. "Not now, then, but we will talk about this at some point."

Mum sighs. "Okay."

She places a hand on the small of my back, urging me to move in the direction of the clubhouse. Every instinct should be screaming at me not to go through those doors, but for the first time in months I feel safe, like this is where I'm supposed to be. I don't understand it, but I've learned to trust my instincts since I was taken by the Jesters.

I meet Howler's eyes. He's standing just a few feet behind us, his other brothers flanking him, but there's nothing hostile in that formation. I don't think any of these men intend to harm us.

"Pia, you are safe here. I would never have brought you here if you weren't," Mum says, cupping my face as she does. I lean into her touch, unable to stop myself from doing so. It's the first time in a long time someone has touched me without anger or without hurting me. "You can trust these men. They are like family."

I want to ask my mother how she is involved in the MC, how she knows these men well enough to call them family, but I feel Gavin's hand on my back, pushing me towards the front doors.

My hand slips into Mum's, needing reassurance that I am finally free from the hell I have been living, needing the assurance that she is real and not some conjuring of my mind.

As soon as we're inside, my eyes roam around the hallway we stepped into. There are multiple doors leading off it, and a set of double doors at the bottom.

The building is quiet, so different from the Jesters. There was a nonstop party going on, with never a moment of peace to be heard within those walls, and not just because there was a constant turntable of men waiting to use me.

The room he takes us into has a sofa pushed up against one wall and a large double bed in the centre of the space. The furniture looks worn, but not in a state of disrepair. There's a mini fridge under the window and a large TV on the wall opposite the bed. The smell of cigarette smoke lingers in the air, as if it's infused in the very material of the room.

"There's a bathroom through that door there. It's only got a shower, no bath, but it should be enough for you to clean up." Gavin stares at me for a moment and I wonder what is going through his head. Then he shakes himself before he speaks again. "I'll get you some clean clothes. Some food too."

I stare at him as if he has lost his mind. "Thank you for the rescue, but we're going home, though I will take the offer of clean clothes."

I don't mean home as in the home I shared with Max before he sold me down the river. I mean home as in the childhood home I grew up in with my mother. I need familiarity. I need my mum.

"You can't leave. Wrecker is still out there. It's too dangerous."

"I can handle Wrecker." It's a lie. I could never handle him, but I don't want anyone else to know how vulnerable he made me.

"Wrecker?"

"Jesters' president," Gavin explains to Mum.

Part of me doesn't care that he is out there. I just want to return to a semblance of normality. I need some level of control back in my life after it was all stripped from me. "You can't keep us here."

Gavin steps into my space and I shrink back, unable to stop the fear from crawling through me. The man is huge, bigger than Wrecker, and he managed to overpower me with ease. "I don't want to be a cunt, kid, but until we find this guy you and your mum are not leaving."

I grit my teeth, ready to throw down, but Mum grabs my hands. "Gavin knows what he's doing, sweetheart." She turns to him and gives him a smile that I've never seen her direct at anyone before. It is soft and filled with desire at same time. What the hell is he to her? "We'd appreciate some clothes. And food."

Gavin nods and something passes between them, a silent communication that I can't understand. Then he turns and leaves the room without another word.

I turned to my mother straight away. "Who is he and how the hell are you mixed up with an MC?"

Mum huffs a breath and moves over to the bed, sinking onto the edge of it. "That's a long story."

"We have time."

Her eyes come to mine and I see the dismay in them. "What did they do to you Pia?"

The change in direction of conversation makes me jolt. I don't want to answer this. I don't want to admit how weak I was by letting them do things to me that no human should ever be subjected to. It makes me feel pathetic, the way all my choices were stripped from me. I wind my arms around my middle and turn away, suddenly unable to look her in the eyes. "It doesn't matter."

"It matters, sweetheart."

My skin feels suddenly like it's crawling with ants. I rub my arms, trying to dispel the feeling. "It's over. Done with." The club made sure of that. I didn't watch the fire burning as we drove away, but I didn't need to. I knew the men inside were dead and that the hellhole I'd survived in for months was nothing more than charred ashes. That was enough to loosen the pain in my chest and allow me to breathe freely. Mostly, anyway. Wrecker is still out there, and I have no idea what his retribution will be for burning his clubhouse to the ground. The man has a cruel, wicked streak that honestly at times scared me.

"It doesn't take a genius to work out what happened to you." Tears stand in Mum's eyes, and I hate seeing them. I never wanted to hurt her or upset her, and I find myself cursing Max for putting me in the situation in the first place.

"Yes." The word squeaks out, emotion overcoming me, "Whatever you're thinking happened, whatever terrible scenario you're playing over in your head, it was worse. They tried to break me piece by piece, but I never submitted to them. I fought every moment of every day for my dignity and my respect. Now, I need to shower."

"Pia, no matter what happened to you, we will get through this. I promise."

I want to believe her, but I don't know that I can ever be the same person I was before this happened. I head into the bathroom, sliding the lock into place on the door behind me. I slide down the back of the door to the floor, until my bottom hits the tiles. Then I let the tears flow.

CHAPTER 6
HOWLER

I watch Socket and Valentina from across the common room. They have their heads together, both of their expressions bleak. I don't know how they're supposed to reconcile what happened to their daughter. I wouldn't wish that shit on my worst enemy.

I make a call to Mara, the club's doctor and Trick's old lady. Without question, she agrees to come down to the clubhouse to take a look at Pia. I don't know what kind of damage was done to her by the Jesters, but she is bruised enough and beaten enough that she needs to see someone. We can't risk taking her to the hospital. Too many nosey nurses who will demand to know what happened. That can't be explained without leading a trail back to the burned-out Jesters clubhouse. I'll protect my brothers at any cost. I'm not letting one of them go down for this.

There are a handful of brothers, sitting around small tables on low stools, and the prospect behind the bar. The stereo is letting out a dull moan, but I don't pay the song any attention. Instead my gaze turns to the doors of the common room as they swing open and Pia steps into the room. She is dressed in a pair of old joggers and a T-shirt that hangs off her thin frame. Her damp hair hangs around her face in loose waves. I can't stop from watching her, even though I know I shouldn't. She is Socket's daughter. I shouldn't be thinking of her in any way but familial, but the thoughts that cross my mind are anything but.

I watch as she walks over to her parents, wondering if Socket has told her the truth yet. She deserves to know who she really is, and Socket deserves to know his child. I still can't wrap my head around why he remained hidden from her for so long. Does he truly believe she had a better life not knowing her father?

I push those thoughts aside. It's not my place to judge another brother's choices. Socket did what he did and he had his reasons. I'll support him no matter what.

The conversation between the three of them starts to get heated. Pia's voice raises and I can pick out a few words here and there. Something about home and wanting to leave.

It's not happening.

Wrecker is still out there.

I'll keep her here myself if I have to. I will fucking lock her in a room, chained to the head of the bed, if necessary. She is not leaving. She's not putting herself back in a position where she's in danger.

"Who the hell are you to tell me what I can and can't do?" she yells at Socket.

She sounds exactly like what she is—a daughter arguing with her father. That thought hits me square in the chest.

Throwing her hands up in the air, Pia storms from the room. Socket starts to rise to go after her, but Valentina stops him with a hand on his bicep. He reclaims his seat while I slip out of my own and out of a side door that leads to a small terrace. It's cool outside, the air colder than it should be for the time of year. I make my way around the front of the building and I find Pia sitting on one of the picnic tables near the bike parking area.

As I approach, she gives me a sullen look. "Have you come to tell me that I can't leave, too?"

I lower myself onto the bench next to her, then pull my smokes out from my pocket and offer her one. She draws her brows together before glancing in my direction. "You're a bad influence, do you know that?"

"You don't have to smoke them." I move the packet away from her, but she rolls her eyes as she takes one. I watch as she puts it between cracked and bruised lips. White heat fills my veins as I take in every mark, every bruise covering her skin. We made the Jesters' ends too fucking quick. We should have made them suffer more.

I glance away, gritting my teeth in an attempt to calm the anger boiling through me. I don't have much of a moral code, but there are some lines I would never cross. I don't hurt women or children, unless the women are in the life and know the risks. Pia is innocent. She should never have been brought into this crap.

"Mara is coming down in the next hour. She is Trick's old lady."

I reach over and light her cigarette for her before lighting my own. She takes a drag before turning back to me. "Who are Trick and Mara?"

"Trick is one of my brothers who pulled you into the common room in the Jesters' clubhouse. He had brown hair."

She pulls her lips down into a grimace

"I think I left a few marks on him."

"He can take it," I tell her. He can. Trick is built like a fucking tank. Most of my brothers are.

"Mara's his old lady. She's also a doc."

Pia shakes her head. "I don't need to see a doctor."

Her walls slam down and whatever progress I was making a second ago is lost. I don't know why I care about making shit better for her. I don't know her. Yeah, she's a brother's kid, which makes her family in a way, but it is more than that. For some reason, I want to avenge all her wrongs.

"Understand you might think that, but you look pretty beat up, Pia. You need to be checked over."

She glances away, flicking the ash of the end of her cigarette onto the concrete below. "I've had worse."

Worse?

She looks like hell. How could she have suffered worse than this? I tense my jaw, trying not to let my anger explode, even though it wants to. She shouldn't have suffered any of it. "Saw you arguing with your mum and Socket."

Her mouth pulls into a tight line. "I want to go home. I can't stay here. Not with all these bikers around." Realising she might have offended me, her head snaps up. "I didn't mean… I don't…" She blows out a breath. "I appreciate the hospitality, Howler, but we don't belong here."

She's wrong about that. This is exactly where she belongs. For better or worse, this is her home too. Her family. The Sons will always take fucking care of her. No matter where she is in the country, any of our chapters will protect her.

"We aren't like those Jester fucks."

Her smile is soft, but her eyes are sad. "I can see you're different. You've already shown me more respect and care than I ever got at the hands of Wrecker, but you're still a club. I don't know that I can get around that."

She takes another drag of her cigarette, blowing the smoke away from me. Fuck, that pisses me off. Not because she doesn't trust my club, but because Wrecker made her this way.

"How'd Max get involved with the Jesters?"

She tucks a piece of damp hair behind her ear and I can't stop following the movement. She seems vulnerable, but I see the fire beneath that. The fight. Wrecker tried to destroy her, and while part of her is broken, she is not shattered. I admire that strength. There are plenty of grown men who wouldn't have that resolve.

"Max has always been the kind of man who wants more than he has. He was never content. He wanted a bigger house, a bigger car, better holidays. I didn't care about that stuff. I just wanted him. I had no idea, but he started borrowing money so we could afford things that were outside of our budget."

"Loan sharks?" I guess.

She nods. "They were on the payroll of the Jesters."

"You had no idea he was borrowing?"

She shakes her head, gripping the edge of the picnic bench until her knuckles whiten. "It sounds stupid now when I say it, but Max handled all of our money. I didn't have a clue what we owed and what we didn't, what we could afford and what we couldn't. I knew his job paid well and that he got bonuses. I just assumed we had the cash for all the things he bought. I never imagined for a second he was using a loan shark and that he owed thousands of pounds. Maybe even hundreds of thousands."

The urge to find Max and smack him in his stupid face fills me for a moment. Getting himself into a mess was one thing, but dragging his spouse into it was another.

"Where is Max now?"

"I don't know. Neither did Wrecker. I came home from work one afternoon and all his stuff was gone. He drained our accounts, took all my jewellery and left." She stares into space, her brow heavy. I know the end of the story, how she was taken to pay the debt, but I don't know why. Why had the Jesters chosen to take her instead of hunting down Max?

"Why did Wrecker decide the debt was yours to repay?" She gives me a look that says I'm being fucking nosey. "Need to know what the situation is, darlin', if I'm going to keep you safe."

That seems to soothe her.

"He came to the house. He asked questions about Max that I couldn't answer. The way he looked at me... He took me because he wanted me, not because of Max and what he was owed. He liked what he saw and that's all." She laughs, but there's no humour in it. It is a dark guttural sound that makes my stomach twist. "Wrecker is a man who's used to taking what he wants. He didn't care that I had a life, a family. He wanted me and he took me—end of story."

"You know you can't go home, don't you? Not while he's still out there. I don't know what frame of mind Wrecker is in. I do know if someone had killed my brothers and burnt my clubhouse to the ground there would be nowhere they could hide from me. Wrecker is going to want revenge. It's safer for you and your mum to stay here until we find him or he surfaces. We have ways of protecting you."

Her eyes narrow. "How do you know my mother? And why are you so willing to help us?"

I'm not a man who lies. Truth is truth, no matter who it hurts, but Socket needs to tell her in his own time. "That's not my story to tell."

She huffs out a breath. "I wish everyone would stop treating me like a child who needs to be kept in the dark. I deserve to know what's going on. I deserve to know if your club is going to expect a similar sort of debt repayment from my mother."

I recoil as if she slapped me. After everything I just said, she still believes my club is on the same level as Wrecker's. That's a kick to the fucking balls. "I don't take people in payment. I'm not that much of a bastard."

She has the grace to look sorry for what she said. "Howler... I didn't... I'm sorry. Your club has been good to us, but I spent months being abused by another MC. It's going to take me a while not to see every MC as the enemy."

"Understand that, even if I don't like it. I do understand. My word probably doesn't mean much to you, but I give it anyway. No one will hurt you while you're here."

She gives me a thin smile. "And I'm supposed to just trust you, am I?"

"Trust is earned. But the sentiment stands. You're safe while within these walls. Can't make you stay. No one can. But it ain't smart to be out there while he is."

I watch as she swallows hard, seeing the dismay in her eyes that this isn't over yet. "I'll think about it," she promises.

I want to push her, make her agree to my terms, but I know if I do, she'll bring up those titanium walls that surround her, protecting her from the hurt and the pain that she has suffered.

I stub out my cigarette and shift my shoulders. "You've got to do what you've got to do. But you're welcome here for as long as you need. You and your mum."

I push up from the bench and walk back inside. I'm just about to shove through the door when she speaks again.

"Howler?" I turn back to her. Her tongue darts out and wets her bottom lip and I trace the movement, unable to stop myself. "Thanks."

I give her a slight lift of my chin and then I walk back into the clubhouse.

CHAPTER 7
PIA

I don't know how long I sit outside for, but eventually I head back inside the building, knowing I can't hide forever. When I do, Mum is still sitting at the table with the man who gave me his hoodie—Socket. There's something about the way she has her head close to his that makes my eyes narrow. I've never seen my mother look at anyone the way she's looking at him right now. The softness of her gaze, the little touches she gives him... Is my mum sleeping with a biker?

The idea is so ludicrous I almost laugh out loud, but he is just as gentle with her. I watch as this brute of a man, a walking and talking tank, takes Mum's hand in his and lifts it to his lips, pressing a kiss to the back of her knuckles.

"You must be Pia."

My head snaps around at the voice to the side of me. The woman is tiny, just over five foot, with a pink pixie haircut and numerous earrings running up the shell of her left ear. She is wearing a leather jacket with a band tee underneath. I don't recognise the name, but that's not surprising. I don't listen to a lot of music, preferring to read a book or watch TV. Her jeans are low on her hips, showing off her midriff and her pierced belly button.

"Yeah, I'm Pia." She gives me a warm smile that instantly puts me at ease.

"I'm Mara. Howler asked me to come down."

The last thing I want is a doctor to examine me, to see my shame in every mark and every bruise of my body. "I'm sorry you wasted your time. I don't need a doctor."

Her smile doesn't fade from her face as she gently steers me towards the exit. I'm not sure why my feet are moving, but I let her lead me out into the corridor beyond the common room. She opens the door off the hallway and pushes it open. There is a double bed pushed against the wall and a sofa opposite it. I know precisely what this room is used for.

Fucking.

They had a similar set up in the Jesters clubhouse. I saw my share of club bunnies fucked and hurt in these rooms.

I lick my lips, my heart starting to race in my chest. Mara places a hand on my arm. "It's okay, Pia. You're safe here."

She's wrong. Nowhere is safe. I turn to leave, needing air, my chest constricting so tightly I can hardly draw in oxygen.

I shove through the door, my chest so tight it feels like my heart is going to explode. I slam into a hard body, and

I can't stop the scream that erupts from my mouth. It rolls up my throat like a tidal wave of panic. Strong arms grip my shoulders. I thrash against the hold, terror leaving me gasping for breath.

"It's me, Pia. It's me."

Howler. It's his voice.

It's enough to ground me, and to bring me back from the panic that is circling me. He wraps his arms around me, pulling me close against his chest. He smells so good—the leather of his kutte and the aftershave he's wearing infuse my nose. I don't want to let go of him as I let out heaving sobs. I should care that he's a biker. I should care he could make me disappear with one word to his men, but I feel safe with him. I can't explain it, but there's something about him that calms all my frayed nerves. "I can't... I can't..."

"Then you don't have to."

I cling to his kutte, the leather soft beneath my fingers. My eyes drift to the president's patch on his chest before moving over the other patches covering the leather. There's one saying 'Crow' and a few others that I can't make sense of. Random numbers and letters.

He runs his fingers through my hair before he crushes my face against his chest, making all thoughts of the patches dissipate. For the first time in months, I feel safe.

Howler eases that crushing feeling that makes my heart feel like it's going to stop.

I cling to him, like I'm drowning in a river and he is life-saving driftwood.

He lets me cry for a time, then he pulls me back from

him. I don't release my hold on his kutte, but I do allow him to create space between us. He lifts my chin with his finger, forcing my eyes to his. "Tell me what you need."

Before I can even contemplate my words or the repercussions of them, I say, "You."

His browse twitch together at me. "Believe me, darlin', I'm the last thing you need."

But he's wrong. With him I feel safe. With him I feel like I can breathe for the first time in months. "Please." I'm not sure what I'm begging for, but he nods and takes my hand. He brushes my hair back from my face, his eyes soft.

"What you need is sleep. When's the last time you slept without fucking fear?"

I try to think, but in truth I can't remember a time when I did sleep without fear. It feels like my life has been nonstop torment. Truthfully, I can't remember what life was like before I was taken. It feels like I've been stuck in this perpetual nightmare for so long now.

I'm strung out, exhaustion weighing on my shoulders, but closing my eyes, letting sleep claim me, feels like an impossible feat. How can I sleep and keep watch?

"I'll stay with you," he says, as if he is reading my mind and can see what's haunting me.

"Howler… no."

"Not asking," he says.

He takes my hand and I let him guide me back up the corridor towards the room I was taken to when I first arrived. He opens the door and leads me inside. My heart is still hammering against my ribs as he orders me to get into the bed.

I hesitate for just the briefest second. He notices instantly.

"I can leave if you want me to."

I don't. Being alone would leave me trapped in my thoughts and that's dangerous. If my mind is quiet, it gives me too much time to think. I need to keep occupied. Busy. I need distractions and Howler is just that—a distraction.

I shake my head. "Stay please."

He stares at me for a brief moment and I wonder what's going through his head. Then he nods.

"Okay." I don't know why he agrees. He's the president of a motorcycle club. I'm sure he has better things to do than babysit me. Wrecker would never have done something like this. I don't know much about Howler, other than the few moments we have been together, but I know the kind of men who are drawn to this lifestyle. They're hard, unrelenting and savage. I have no doubt Howler is all of those things and more. He exudes danger when I look at him. His actions told me he's ruthless, too. He ordered those men dead and had listened to those shots ringing out without flinching, even though he knew each shot was ending a man's life. Not that a single member of the Jesters could be considered a man.

But it takes a certain kind of personality to stand by while men are killed.

One without a soul.

One who is trapped in the darkness that this world is grounded in.

No one joined a motorcycle club because they had a good life.

I learnt that the hard way.

There wasn't a single member of the Jesters that wasn't deprived and covered in the filth of their actions.

Wrecker was the worst, but the others were just as bad.

Boulder had taken me against my will repeatedly in the months I was with the Jesters. Griller, too. He'd tied me to the bed one night and used me until I bled. I didn't mourn any of their deaths. They deserved it and more.

But I did worry what it said about Howler and the men in his club.

Am I truly safe here?

I study his face for a moment, not sure that I trust my own judgement any longer. I thought Max was a good man, after all.

"Lie down, darlin'," he says in a low voice that soothes me instantly.

I crawl onto the bed and under the duvet, pulling it up to my chin as I settle against the pillows. He moves to the sofa pushed against the wall and sits on the edge of it, clasping his hands between his open legs.

I lie there, convinced there's no way in hell I can sleep, but after a time my eyes become heavy and I start to drift off.

I don't know how long I'm out for, but I wake screaming, clinging to the blankets. I jack-knife up in bed to find solid hands gripping my shoulders, stopping me from thrashing. "You're okay."

I stop screaming, trying to calm my racing heart down. I feel nauseous; dizzy, too. I cling to Howler's biceps, as if he is the only thing keeping me grounded. "I'm sorry…" I gasp out the words, feeling suddenly self-conscious for my reaction.

"It was just a dream," Howler says. But it isn't just a dream. These nightmares are my reality now. I have to deal with the abuse I suffered, and somehow I have to put my broken pieces back together so I can continue to have a life. I don't know how to do that. It seems impossible. I close my eyes and let a tear escape from the corner. I hate Max, for what he did, for the way he left me to deal with his mess. I hate myself for choosing a man like that, for not really seeing who he was. I put my trust in him. I loved him. It is clear he never felt a single thing for me. If he had, he would never have been able to leave me like that. He had to know what Wrecker would do.

Brushing my hair back, Howler scans every inch, every line of my face. "I'll find him," he promises. "There's nowhere that fucker can hide from the Sons."

"Max?"

"Wrecker. Though, if you want to find your husband I can do that too."

"Ex-husband," I correct. There is nothing Max could say to me that would make me want to stay with him. He can't fix the wrongs he has made. And there is no amount of glue in the world that is going to put me back together again the way I was before I was taken.

I really hope that is a promise he can keep. Because knowing Wrecker is out there scares me more than anything. When I was with the Jesters he had control. He liked it. Craved that power. Now, he is in the wind, his empire crumbled around him, and his brother is dead. I have no idea what he will do, and that fucking terrifics me.

"I know you're scared. I understand why, so this is the last time I'll bring it up. See Mara. Let her examine you, maybe even see about getting someone for you to talk to about what happened." He runs his fingers over my jaw, so delicately, so unlike any touch I've ever had before.

I want to deny his request, but he's been good to me. "Okay," I agree quickly before I change my mind. "I hope you know what you did by destroying the Jesters. Wrecker won't take this lying down."

"Let me worry about that bastard. All you need to focus on is you."

I hope his club hasn't bitten off more than it can chew, because Wrecker can be a spiteful prick when he wants to be, but I have to trust Howler. Right now, he is the only thing standing between me and that maniac. Wrecker is still out there somewhere, and knowing him as I do, he will be hell-bent on getting revenge

CHAPTER 8
HOWLER

I lean back in my seat, threading the gavel between my fingers as I listen to Socket's update on Wrecker. It's been two days since we brought Pia to the clubhouse. She hasn't mentioned leaving again, fear that the Jesters' former president is still out there making her hesitant to go home. At least here, within the walls of the clubhouse, she knows she is safe. Or at least I hope she knows that by now.

Pia let Mara examine her and give her some painkillers. She didn't confirm what had gone on, but I didn't need the doc to tell me that Pia had been raped. Didn't need an exam report, either. It was written in every twitch and tremble of her body. In the way she held herself. I hated seeing that fucking shame in her eyes, like it was hers to bear. She deserved better.

I'd never say it to Socket, but if he'd claimed her as his daughter, this shit would never have happened. She'd have had club protection from her first fucking breath and those Jester fucks might have given pause before touching her.

My brother has enough guilt pressing on his shoulders, though, so I keep those thoughts to myself.

"That fuck is in the wind," Socket says, bringing my attention back to the conversation. I curve my fingers into fists, digging the nails into my palms until I feel the half-moon shapes left behind.

I rap my knuckles against the table, my ire growing. "We need to find him, and fast."

For Pia, but for the club, too. It's dangerous having an enemy out there, gunning for us.

Fucking Wrecker.

That cunt has done the ultimate disappearing act since we raided his fucking clubhouse. I don't know how he got out of the clubhouse when my men swarmed it, but somehow that slippery fuck vanished into thin air. The fact that he left his men to die while he escaped told me what kind of president he was.

He was a bastard and a coward.

A man who preyed on those weaker than him.

A man who left those he was supposed to lead to die.

The captain should have gone down with his ship.

Yet he fled like one of the rats on board, saving his own skin while he condemned others to death.

That left a sour taste in my mouth.

I didn't like the Jesters. Didn't like a single thing their club stood for, but if the head is rotten, the body dies.

Wrecker was rotten to the core and that filtered down to the fuckers he had under him.

With a different man at the helm, the fate of the Road Jesters might have had a different ending.

That fucker should have stood with his brothers. He should have died in that building, on his knees, like a man. He should have faced his death with dignity.

The reaper comes for us all, especially in this life. Nothing is guaranteed. Tomorrow might not be on the cards for any one of us. You can't dance with death daily and not get dragged down to hell at some point. I play Russian roulette with my life every time I pull my kutte onto my back, as do the men I lead.

It's part of the job.

An expectation of the lifestyle.

Terror leans forwards, his broad shoulders blocking out Brewer, who is sitting next to him. "I'll talk to some contacts again. Some fucker out there knows something."

I doubt there'll be any talking involved. Terror doesn't know how to use his words. He's all about the fucking violence, which is why he's perfect as my sergeant at arms.

"I'll shake a few branches too," Blackjack says. "See what falls out of the tree. You want to call Ravage in on this?"

I give my VP my attention. The London chapter president of the Sons would ride to us in an instant if I picked up the phone and asked him.

I don't think we need help yet though, and I prefer to

handle my shit in-house. Rav sent me here to set up the Manchester chapter because he trusted me. I don't want to call him for every little incident.

"No; for now, keep looking. If we need resources from our national brothers we can always ask for it."

I dismiss the brothers, ordering Socket to wait behind. My brother stays in his seat as the room empties of my officers. Once the door is shut, I slide my eyes towards him.

"You ever planning on telling Pia that you're her father?" It's not what I intended to say and the words are sharper than they should be. It makes Socket sit up straight in his seat. I don't know why I'm getting involved in another brother's business, but it fucking grates on me that she's still in the dark. It isn't right.

His expression is guarded, his body tense as he meets my gaze. "With all due respect, prez, don't remember asking for your opinion."

He is well within his rights to tell me to fuck off. I should back down, but instead his words add fire to the oil swirling around me. "She has a right to know."

Socket looks like he's debating jumping over the table and thumping me in the face. I'd deserve it, too. This isn't my business. Socket can do whatever the fuck he wants to, but I feel this... connection with Pia. A need to keep her safe, even from her own fucking father.

"She's been through literal hell, Howler. She hasn't said it, but I know that cunt raped her. Maybe the whole fucking club did." Socket's lips pull into a snarl making him look feral. My own are probably doing the same, because hearing him say what we all suspect hits me in the chest like a wrecking ball. She allowed Mara to look at her wounds, but when she asked Pia if she was raped Pia didn't say a word. Her silence was a confirmation in my mind. I didn't need the words. I saw her state of undress, the bruises on her thighs. I knew what those animals did to her, without her explicitly saying it.

It made me want to kill Wrecker all the more.

It made me want to set fire to the fucking world. When I'd stayed with her in the room, she'd tossed and turned the whole night before jerking awake. I don't think she'll sleep a full night again for a long time and that also pisses me off.

Socket rubs a hand over his mouth, sadness clouding his eyes. "Made my peace with the fact I'll never know the truth about what really happened to my kid; she's never gonna tell me. Don't like it, but I understand it. But I don't need the words from her. I already know what happened in that fucking clubhouse. I know what those fucking bastards did to her. You can see it in her eyes; the brokenness, the pieces that can't be put back together by me or her mother.

"I don't know Pia, not really. Valentina kept me up to date with general things that were happening and sent photographs, but it ain't the same as knowing someone. Despite that, I can see how she is suffering. I can tell every day is a fucking chore for her. I can see how hard she's fighting against her fucking demons. You think it's the right time for me to dump on her that I'm her father?" He arches a brow. He has a point, but there's never going to be a good time. "I chose not to be in her life, for better or worse; I made that decision. I'd go to the ends of the earth to keep her safe, but I can't tell her who I am. I can't just jump back into her life as if I never left it. Ain't right. She's twenty-fucking-six, Howler. It's been too long."

His voice sounds shredded raw as he speaks and his obvious pain hits me in the fucking gut. He wants to be there for her, I can see it in his eyes. He wants desperately to be her father. "I don't think there's a time limit on becoming someone's dad," I say.

Socket scrubs a hand over his face, and I realise how tired my brother looks. "She deserves better."

"Don't know a man better than you, Socket," I say in a quiet voice.

Socket goes silent for a moment, as if letting my words sink in. "If I was a better man she wouldn't have gotten hurt."

"How the fuck could you have known any of that shit would have played out as it did?"

"If I was in her life I would have chased off that Max prick before he got her involved with the fucking Jesters. I wish she'd talk to someone."

"When she's ready, she will."

Socket's eyes go to the window, narrowing as his lips tighten.

"I want that cunt found, Howler, and I want him when we do."

I want to argue for a brief moment, tell him that he's

mine, but Pia is his daughter. I don't have any claim to her.

Yet.

The thought sits on the tip of my tongue. Yet.

Fuck.

I need to nip those thoughts in the bud before Socket discovers I'm thinking about his daughter like this.

"You can have him," I promise. I can imagine the kind of punishment Socket will mete out on Wrecker. My brother isn't usually the first in line for bleeding a man, but this is his kid. He'll never scrub the image of her in that room from his eyes, no matter what he does. That shit'll haunt him forever. Wrecker will suffer. Even if Socket can't do it, I will. I'll bleed that cunt and cut off his dick for what he did.

I get to my feet and clamp my hand on his shoulder. "We'll find him."

"Soon. Don't like him being out there. Pia isn't safe while he is."

"She's safe in the clubhouse, Socket. Her and Valentina." I don't tell him they can stay as long as they need to. He knows it.

His eyes soften. "Thanks for having my back."

"Always. You know that."

He does. We're not bound by blood, but the men in this clubhouse are as close as blood to me.

Socket and I make our way into the common room. As I enter, I scan the space, taking in brothers and a couple of club bunnies playing pool with Trick and another member, Granger. Two of the girls we brought from the Jesters' clubhouse are clearing glasses, chatting as they do.

My gaze stops at the window.

Pia is sitting outside on the deck, her hair blowing in the breeze, making her look ethereal. She seems lost in her thoughts, staring out over the garden area, which is surrounded by high brick walls, keeping the world back. Considering the wall she's built around herself, it's fitting.

I go to the door that leads outside and I push through it. Pia's head comes up as I let the door go. "We've got to stop meeting like this," she says, her lips curving up at the corners. I can still see the sadness in her eyes, but fuck if that smile doesn't change her whole face. She holds out a packet of cigarettes. "I owe you a few."

I sit next to her on the bench and take the packet, slipping one out. She hands me the lighter when I put it between my lips.

"Never smoked before… this. It's a good excuse to get some alone time. My mother hasn't stopped trying to smother me since I got here."

"She's worried."

"I'm fine."

That's a lie. She's not in the same ballpark as fine. I don't know her that well, but even I can see she looks exhausted.

"You aren't sleeping." Even if I hadn't witnessed her nightmares, it's obvious she's not. There are dark smudges under her eyes.

"I was kidnapped and held hostage for months. I think everyone needs to cut me some slack." She snatches the packet of cigarettes up and pulls one out. "Now, I'm a prisoner here, too."

"You're not a prisoner."

"So, I can leave?"

"No."

"So I am a prisoner," she grumbles. "I need things from my house. My own clothes, my stuff."

"Ain't happening."

I don't bother reiterating the reasons she can't leave. She already knows Wrecker is out there and that she's in danger while he is.

"I can't keep wearing Socket's clothes."

"You need shit; just say. Club'll get it for you." She glances away and I wonder what's going through her head. "What?"

"I don't like being in your club's debt. I'm sure at some point you're going to want repaying."

I can't tell her why that won't happen, not without spilling Socket's secret. "Don't want nothing back, Pia."

She scoffs. "Men like you don't do things for nothing."

"Men like me?"

She swallows hard. "I just meant—"

"Ain't a saint, darlin'. Never professed to being one, but I don't kick people when they're down, either."

She ducks her head, a smile playing across her face. "I think you're sweeter than you pretend to be, Howler."

I snort. No one has ever called me fucking sweet. "Doubtful."

"Your accent isn't local."

"I was born and raised in London. Lived there my whole fucking life."

"What made you move to Manchester?" Her genuine interest in my life fucking surprises me. Most women just care about the patch on my back and what it can give them.

"Got an offer I couldn't refuse." She gives me a look that says *explain*. "I got the chance to be president. To lead my own men." There were a hundred other reasons, but that was the main one. I was outgrowing London. "Don't get me wrong, I love my brothers there, but I wasn't built to follow. Ravage saw that. He recognised the drive in me, the need to create something from nothing."

"You enjoy it?"

"Yeah," I admit. "It ain't always plain sailing, but I've got a good group of men—loyal to the patch and fucking honourable. I trust every one of them with my life."

It hasn't been easy to get where we are. Numerous wars, numerous men dead, but things are settled now. We're in a good place. Most of the smaller gangs are gone or allied with us. I'm keeping an eye on the civil war happening in the Wood syndicate, as their men fight for the top spot, but I'm not worried about those fuckers either. Jeremiah Wood didn't leave a suitable candidate behind to step into his shoes, which has opened his organisation up to a blood bath. Members of the syndicate are being knifed in the street, some cut down with machetes and other weapons.

I'm content to let those cunts kill each other until there's nothing left to fight over.

"What about you?" I ask. "What did you do before?"

"Before I was taken prisoner by a psychotic biker?" Her smile is sad. "I didn't do anything. Max didn't want me to work. He wanted me to be the perfect housewife. He wanted to start a family, but I wasn't ready. He didn't know I kept the implant." She glances down. "Is it wrong that I'm glad? The thought of being tied to him because of a child makes my skin crawl."

I shake my head. "We'll find that cunt, too."

"I don't care about Max. He can rot in hell."

"Good, because that fuck ain't getting near you again."

Her eyes meet mine. "What are you going to do with him when you find him?"

"He sold you down the river, babe. Ain't going to greet him with a fucking hug."

She shakes her head. "Max is a bastard, but he had no idea what Wrecker would do."

"He knew he was leaving you to face his mistakes. That shit can't be forgiven."

"I never said anything about forgiveness. Just…don't kill him."

Despite everything she's been through, Pia is too good, too kind. I can't fathom forgiving someone for the months of abuse she suffered. I can't imagine caring about the fate of the man who put me in that situation either.

But Pia does.

"Can't make any promises," I tell her truthfully. I have no idea what my reaction—or her father's—will be to facing the fucker.

She pushes up from the bench and leans down to kiss

my cheek. Fuck. Her lips are like silk against my skin and I want to pull her around to claim her mouth. I do nothing. I sit and take what she's offering, knowing it could be the only thing she can ever offer me.

"Thank you."

I watch her walk back into the clubhouse and I resist the urge to follow her. Fuck.

CHAPTER 9
PIA

As I step back into the clubhouse, I can't help but cringe at myself. I just kissed Howler. On the cheek. Like he's some schoolboy who defended my honour and not a biker who has probably spilt more blood than I can fathom.

I don't know why he doesn't scare me.

He is a biker.

Like Wrecker.

A man who lives outside the law.

I know exactly who these men are—or at least, I thought I did.

Howler isn't like the Jesters.

The men of his club are different, too.

I don't worry about walking around the clubhouse, no matter the time of day or night. I don't worry about any of the men touching me without permission, either. The first few days I was on edge every time I left the room I'm staying in. That faded when I realised no one within these walls plans on taking me without permission. No one will push me up against a wall and shove inside me. No one will touch my intimate parts when I'm sitting next to them, just because they can.

Strangely, everyone has been polite.

Kind, even.

That's not to say sex isn't happening. It is and it does. Today is no different. As I move through the common room, I pass a sofa where one of the brothers, Terror, I think his name is, has a club bunny on his lap. He's playing absently with her breasts, which are pulled out of her top, as he talks on his phone. As if it's the most natural thing in the world. I try to push down thoughts of my own abuse, of how the men of the Jesters would grope me without permission whenever I was in their common room. I search for any sign the woman is suffering or uncomfortable.

She's not holding back tears; she's not begging him to stop. She's not being slapped or hit. She's biting her bottom lip, her head thrown back, her eyes closed.

Ecstasy.

She's enjoying what he's doing and she's consented to it. When his hand slips down her belly and into her shorts she even widens her thighs to give him the room he needs to finger-fuck her.

That is the difference.

Consent.

She wants this.

I tuck my hair behind my ear and scan the room, ignoring her moans. My mother is sitting with Socket.

Again.

I'm convinced now that there is something going on between them. I can see it in the lines of their bodies. They're close without touching, sitting next to each other at the table, rather than across, as you would if you were with a stranger. His hand is on the top of the table, inches from hers. As if he wants to reach out and take it.

I can't imagine Mum dating a biker in her past, but they look like a couple. The soft look in his eyes when he looks at her confirms it.

Is that why Howler is letting us stay?

Is that why we're not in the club's debt for helping us?

I go to the table and both of them cut off what they are saying to glance up at me.

"I need to talk to my mum," I tell him.

"Pia!" Mum exclaims at my rudeness. It seems strange that she cares about my manners considering Terror is now off the phone and eating that bunny out. No one even looks in their direction, even though she's making little whimpers of pleasure.

"I can do it in front of him, if you'd rather."

Socket pushes to his feet. "It's okay, V. I've got shit to do anyway."

V?

That seems friendly and confirms my suspicions.

He stands and peers down at me, his mouth as soft as his eyes. He's always sweet with me and I don't understand it. From the moment he gave me his hoodie it's like he feels this connection to me—not a romantic one, but maybe some sort of saviour complex. I don't know.

"How are you doing, kid?"

I wake every night drenched in sweat and swallowing a silent scream.

I don't say that.

I force a smile instead. "I'm fine."

His expression tells me he doesn't believe it, but he doesn't push, either. "I'll be around if you need anything."

I wait for him to walk away before I slip into the chair opposite Mum.

"You could be nicer to him."

I narrow my eyes. "You and Socket have history. How do you know him?"

She huffs out a breath. "Okay, fine. Yes I know Gavin. He and I dated a long time ago."

I mull this over. Mum never seemed wild. She was always so focused on making sure I was okay. Her and a biker doesn't make sense to me. "How long ago?"

"What does it matter?"

"I'm trying to understand why your ex-boyfriend would run to the rescue of your daughter."

Mum shifts in her seat and I can see how uncomfortable my questions are making her. It makes me want to push harder. Mum knows me better than anyone on the planet, but that works both ways. I know her, too. She's hiding something from me. Something more than dating a biker.

"Because I asked him to."

"I don't remember him ever being in your life, Mum, so it must have been when I was really young or not born."

She waves a hand and I can see how flustered she is by my questions. "Pia, I don't want to talk about this."

"I need to know you haven't made a deal with the devil. What did you have to do to get me back?" I demand, starting to feel the edge of hysteria creeping up on me. There's no such thing as a good deed done for free. I won't be in the debt of another MC. I doubt Howler would expect the same repayment as Wrecker. The little I know about the Sons president tells me he isn't like that, but no good deed is ever done for free.

The question is, what will he want?

"It isn't like that," she says.

"Then what is it like? Because I'm thinking the worst here, Mum."

"He and I were close," she blurts out. "There was a time when I thought he was it for me, Pia. I loved him deeply."

Her words cut a path through my anger. Tears brim in her eyes and she glances away to hide them, but she can't disguise the swipe of her cheek to catch one that falls. Fuck, I never wanted to make my mother cry. I reach out and grab her hand, needing to comfort her. She trembles in my grasp, but she doesn't pull away.

"What happened?" I ask, softening my voice. I need answers. I need to know if we should be thinking about leaving, even with Wrecker out there on the loose.

She doesn't speak for a moment, her eyes locked on our hands clasped together. "We were young. We had foolish dreams." The whispered words crush my chest as if an anvil has been placed on it. "We just rented a house together. We were making plans for our future. It was the first time in my life I ever felt truly free." She sighs, a contented little sound that makes my gut twist. How did she lose that? "It was…it was good. *He* was good."

"What changed?"

"He got locked up." Her words shouldn't surprise me. They don't. Men like Socket skirt the law all the time. Sometimes it catches up with them. I lean forwards to listen.

"What for?"

"That's a long and complicated story, honey."

I peer across the room to where Gavin is sitting with Howler and another brother, Blackjack. My eyes skim from Gavin, focusing on Howler without meaning to. His gaze rises suddenly, locking on to me.

The way he looks at me makes my breath catch in my throat. I've never been looked at like that by anyone—not Max, not any of my exes. It's so intense, so needy. I don't know if he realises he's doing it.

My heart starts to pound as I force my gaze back to Mum, tearing away from Howler.

The last thing I need is to turn the head of another biker, though Howler is gorgeous, even with that dark edge to him. I need to focus on myself, on trying to repair the pieces of me that Wrecker broke.

"By the time he got out, I knew we could never pick up where we left off," she says, and I realise I missed a little of what she was saying. "He didn't think he was good enough for us."

The way her voice breaks shatters my heart. She loved

him. Truly, deeply loved him. I can hear it in every word, see it in every shattered piece of her expression.

I reach out and grab her hand. "I'm sorry, Mum."

She waves this off. "It's in the past, honey."

"You want him still," I guess.

She gives me a sad smile. "Gavin and I can't ever be together. We're too different now. Our lives have taken different paths. I don't have it in me to be someone's old lady. Not anymore."

"But you love him."

She swallows hard. "Yes. I'll always love him."

"That's why he agreed to help you get me back." I risk glancing back in Howler's direction, but he's got his head close to Blackjack, talking. I'm relieved to escape his stare, but also I want it back—crave it even.

"No." She closes her eyes as pain crawls over her face. I hate seeing it. Growing up it was just the two of us. I never wanted for anything, but I could always tell Mum was lonely. I naively thought, as a kid, that she never met anyone else because she was too busy taking care of me. Now, I realise she had this epic love she couldn't move on from. "There are things you don't know, Pia. Things I can't tell you."

My heart starts to pound in my chest at her words and unease prickles through me. "Like what? Mum, you can tell me anything."

"You'll hate me when I do. I can't." She gets up from the table and darts from the room, leaving me sitting alone, confused by what just happened.

My gaze goes back to the table, but this time to Gavin

—Socket. I can't believe him and my mum had this epic romance, and I can't believe she's never mentioned it before. It's clear she still loves him, and he loves her too. He must have ridden into the Jesters to save me just because she asked it.

But what would I hate her for?

Why is she so sure I would?

I don't care that she had a fling with a motorcycle club member.

I don't care that she never told me until now.

Why would she think either of those things would make me hate her?

Once again, my heart rate starts to pick up. Did she lie about what it cost her to recover me?

I despise being in the dark. Max kept me ignorant for so many years and look where that ended.

I'm going to find out what Mum is hiding. Even if it will destroy us both.

CHAPTER 10
HOWLER

I can't get Pia out of my fucking head. For days she's been walking around the clubhouse in tight leggings and vest tops that leave little to the imagination. I should have sent Mara to get her clothes, not Lissa. The bunny dressed Pia in clothes that showcase every fucking curve of her body. It's driving me crazy.

I've done my best to avoid Socket's kid—as much as I can, considering she's under the same roof as me. I shouldn't be looking at Pia—she's been through hell—but I can't get her out of my fucking mind. I admire that stone-cold resilience she has and the protective streak over her mother, even though she's the one who needs protecting right now.

"It's time to talk to Rav," I say.

Blackjack, who's sitting next to me, glances over. "He's going to want to send brothers."

"We don't need them." Not yet. Maybe not ever.

I am adept at handling shit in-house these days.

"You'll have to convince him of that."

I pat my brother's shoulder before I head out into the garden at the back of the clubhouse and I sit on one of the benches. We have most of our parties back here. There's a brick barbecue set up near one of the perimeter walls and several picnic tables. With families and brothers it can feel busy, but we don't have any more space. The clubhouse is in the middle of the city, so we're lucky to have outdoor space at all.

I dial Rav's number and place the phone to my ear.

"Brother," he says when he answers.

"Hey. How's it going?"

"Sasha's pregnant." Sasha is his old lady and the mother of his other two kids, Lily-May and Jasper.

"Congrats brother."

"Yeah." He clears his throat, but I can tell he's choked up by the news. "Still fucking reeling from it. Jasper was supposed to be our last."

"We'll have a drink to celebrate next time I'm in London," I tell him.

"Was this a social call or did you need something?" he asks.

I rub a hand over my temple which suddenly starts to ache. "Just keeping you up to date with shit. Had a misunderstanding with a colleague. It might escalate. It might not."

I hedge my words in case unfriendly ears are listening on the other end. The pigs usually leave us alone, but it pays to be cautious.

"What kind of misunderstanding?"

"The kind where he took a brother's daughter off his hands."

Ravage is silent for a moment, but knowing him as well as I do, I know he's silently fuming. When he speaks his words are sharp. "You bring her home?"

"Yeah. He's still out there, though."

"Pissed?"

"I'd say so." We burnt his clubhouse to the ground and killed every person inside the walls. I'd say he's furious.

"I was thinking of taking a ride up to Manchester."

I shake my head. "Not that I wouldn't be pleased to see you, brother, but it ain't necessary. Not yet."

"It becomes necessary you pick up the phone and I'll be there."

This is where the bonds of brotherhood come into their own. You don't fight one Son. You fight us all.

If I need it, Rav will ride north will as many men as he can spare. He'll call on reinforcements from other chapters of the Sons that are closer to us, too—like Birmingham and Leicester.

"Will do."

I hang up.

I need to get rid of some energy. I need to stop thinking about Socket's fucking daughter. I go to the end of the garden. There's a block of wood attached to the wall with a target painted on it. I pull a knife from my boot and throw it. It whistles through the air before it hits the target and quivers.

I step up to the block and pull it free before going back to the same position and throwing it again.

For the second time, it hits the target.

"Are you aiming at anyone in particular?"

I snap my head around to see Pia standing behind me. She looks fucking stunning. She's in a pair of thick red leggings and she's wearing a cropped sweater that shows off her midriff. Her hair is loose around her shoulders, tumbling down her back, and her makeup-free face looks more refreshed than I've seen her since she got here.

"You sleeping better?" I don't know what possesses me to ask it. She seems just as surprised by my question.

"Uh...not really, but your friend Mara gave me some sleeping tablets. They work wonders." She steps up to me. "You still haven't answered who you're aiming at."

She's so close I can smell her bodywash. Strawberries maybe. It's sweet as fuck. I want to pull her into me and inhale her, but I force my feet to keep still. "You think I have a list of enemies I work my pent up rage out on?"

"You mean you don't?"

I laugh. Me. I don't laugh, but she brings this shit out in me. "No."

If I have an enemy, I put them down. Fast. It was how I came to own the city centre. I was ruthless in the early days. I had to be, to carve out our own little kingdom. There were gangs entrenched in the area who didn't want us invading their patch. I understood it. I would have been the same. It's why we destroyed them first.

I'm pissed at myself for not seeing the threat the Road Jesters still posed. They were far enough outside of our patch not to be a problem. If they hadn't taken Pia, I doubt they would have been an issue still.

"That surprises me."

"I don't give my enemies much fucking thought," I admit.

She stares at the knife in the board for a moment. "Can I try?"

"You want to throw?"

"Yeah." She arches a brow. "You think I can't do it?"

The challenge in her voice makes me smirk. "Darlin', I don't think there's a single thing you can't do."

Colour rises in her cheeks as she dips her head. "There's plenty of things I can't do, Howler."

I place a finger under her chin, forcing her head up. "Don't do that."

"Do what?" she asks, meeting my gaze.

"Hide."

"I'm not."

I want to dip my head and claim her mouth so badly, but I force my body to still. She isn't ready for anything yet.

Pia's eyes crawl over mine and I can see there is heat building behind her lashes. She shakes herself.

"Show me how to throw?"

It's a bad idea, but I go to the block and pull my knife free. I make my way back to Pia and hand her the knife.

"Is there a secret to it?"

She stands, holding the knife ready to throw. "Just aim and let it go."

She does and it hits the block but doesn't stick into the wood. Instead, it clatters to the ground.

The disappointment in her face makes me want to bleed someone. "That was terrible," she says.

"You're learning. It takes time."

I retrieve the knife and bring it back to her. "You've got to relax your body." I stand behind her, my chest moulded against her back, and I grab her hand so I can position her. She jolts beneath me, her breath catching. This isn't an intake of breath that tells me she's interested. She's fucking scared.

Her breath tears out of her. Instantly I release her. "Fuck," I mutter. I didn't think.

Pia licks her lips and drags her fingers through her hair. "I'm sorry."

"You don't need to apologise."

"I thought…it's just…I was in that room again."

I don't know what room she's talking about, but it doesn't matter. She's fucking freaked, and that's enough.

"I shouldn't have touched you."

Pia closes her eyes, as if she's trying to ground herself. "Am I going to be like this forever? Twitching every time someone touches me unexpectedly?"

"Things will get better," I promise her. "Pia, they raped you. Brutally. It ain't something you just put aside."

Her whole body flinches at my words, but she doesn't deny it either. "It helps knowing most of them are dead."

The coldness in her words doesn't surprise me. It's the candour that does. It's the first time she's admitted she was raped.

"We'll get Wrecker, too."

"He was the worst," she says, wrapping her arms around her middle.

"He'll die the worst then," I vow.

Her eyes snap up to mine. "You talk about death as if it is nothing."

"Ain't sorry to kill a man who hurt an innocent, Pia."

Her tongue dips out and wets her bottom lip. "I want him dead, too, and I can't reconcile with that. Good people don't wish harm to others. But the things he did to me…" She shivers. "I don't want him to ever do that to anyone else."

I want to reach out and take her hands, but after her reaction I don't want to touch her again.

"He won't."

"Yeah…" She seems to shake off her maudlin thoughts. "So my mum and Socket apparently had this huge epic love story. Did you know about it?"

This time I'm the one freezing. "They tell you that?"

"Mum did. I kind of guessed too. The way they were together…it was clear there was something between them."

"Known Socket a long time."

"Did you know him when he and my mum were together?" She reaches out, her fingers scraping over my hand as she takes the knife from me. It makes me want to capture her mouth like a starved man.

"No."

I don't like the path this questioning is taking. I don't want to lie to her. Ain't my way to do that, but Socket is my brother. I owe him my loyalty more than Pia. For whatever reason, my brother has decided to keep this shit from her. Who am I to tell him it's wrong?

"She said he went to prison. That was what stopped their relationship."

"So Socket told me."

She launches the knife at the block but it hits and clatters to the ground again.

"It must have been some relationship for him to fight as hard as he did to get me home."

I retrieve the knife, unease slithering through me. "Socket's fucking loyal to those he cares about."

"Loyal enough to go into danger for a woman he hasn't seen in twenty-plus years?" Her brow arches. "You have to admit that's weird."

"Socket cares about your mum."

She glances down at the knife I offer back to her. "Would you do it for an old girlfriend?"

"Depends on the ex."

Pia takes the knife and launches it at the target. This time it sticks in the wood with a thwack. It's off target, but it hit.

Her mouth opens wide as she shrieks her excitement. Then without warning, throws her arms around my neck. It takes me off balance, but I wrap my arms around her, pulling her against me. Fuck, she feels amazing in my arms, like the sweetest treat. I take in her smell, wanting nothing more than to push her onto the nearest bench and sink balls-deep into her pretty cunt.

But she's Socket's kid.

She's also been through hell.

This ain't right.

I carefully untangle her hold on my neck and pull back from her. She's still smiling. "I hit it!"

"Yeah, darlin', you did." Fuck, my balls feel like they're being strangled as I peer down at her. She felt perfect in my arms and I wish she was still there.

Pia stares up at me. "Practice makes perfect, right?"

I want to kiss her. It takes all my willpower to stop from dipping my head and claiming her mouth. I've never been a man who let shit go. I take what I want.

I want her, have from the moment I saw her in that fucking room, but it isn't right. She's not in a place to be thinking about this shit.

So I do the only thing I can. "Keep going. I got shit to do."

"Your knife."

"Keep it," I mutter before I make my escape.

CHAPTER 11
PIA

I jolt upright in bed, screaming. Fear clutches my heart, making my spine snap straight even as it drenches me in sweat. All my synapses tingle with adrenaline as I blink into the inky darkness of the room.

Fuck.

The nightmare was the same as always.

I was in the room with Wrecker. He was raping me while Griller and Boulder awaited their turns.

I scramble to switch the bedside lamp on and the room floods with light. Fuck, I can't keep doing this.

Shaking, I climb out of bed and move to the adjoining bathroom. I run the tap, ignoring the mirror hanging over the sink, not wanting to see my face. I don't want to see the tiredness or the broken pieces in my eyes.

I splash water on my face, before I lean against the ceramic. My pulse is still racing even though I'm trying to take calm, steadying breaths.

I use the toilet, wash my hands and head back into the

bedroom. For a moment, I sit on the edge of the bed, trying to regain control.

I need a drink. Something alcoholic.

I grab a sweater and pull it on over the tee I was wearing for bed, then find a pair of joggers and put them on too before I make my way down to the common room.

It's late, early hours of the morning, so the clubhouse is quiet. I expect to see the lights off, but the common room is lit up. When I push through the doors, there's a prospect at the bar. I think his name is Freddy.

I move to the bar and slide onto a stool in front of it. There are a handful of brothers sitting around tables, deep in conversation. Terror is passed out on one of the sofas, two bunnies sprawled over him. That man is a horn dog.

Freddy moves over to me. "What can I get you?"

"Vodka. Neat."

He moves away and starts to make the drink.

"Why are you awake?" a voice says from behind me. I turn to see Howler behind me.

"I could ask you the same thing."

"I don't sleep."

"What, ever?" I raise a brow. "Are you human?"

He smiles and I like it when he does. It takes that severity out of his expression. "There are plenty of people who don't think so."

They would be wrong. I see Howler's humanity every time he talks to me. I don't know if it's intentional or not, but it's there.

"They're wrong."

"Be careful, darlin'. I've got a reputation to uphold. So why you down here?"

Freddy deposits the glass in front of me. It's not a bar measure in the glass. It's more than four fingers worth of vodka. I take the tumbler and knock it back, relishing the burn as it hits my throat. I slip the glass back onto the bar top.

"You looking to get drunk?"

"Depends," I say.

"On?"

"Whether you're joining me."

He sighs. "Darlin'..."

"Have a drink with me, Howler. It won't kill you."

I think he's going to say no, but then he signals to Freddy who starts to make him a drink.

"Why are you awake?" he asks again.

"Couldn't sleep."

"Because?"

"Well, after you're held hostage for months, sleep doesn't come easily." I shouldn't be so flippant, but I can't help it. If I don't make light of the situation, I'll spiral into a deep hole I'm not sure I'll be able to climb out of.

Howler surprises me by cupping my jaw. His hand is warm, rough, and I want to lean into it. I shouldn't, but I allow myself this small pleasure, rubbing against his palm like a cat.

"The club paid in blood for what they did. Wrecker will pay too, I promise."

"I know."

He rubs his thumb over the apple of my cheek. "You need to sleep, darlin'. I can see how tired you are."

"The nightmares come when I'm alone." Admitting that makes me flush. I don't want him to see me as weak, but that's exactly how I feel.

Howler signals to Freddy. "The bottle."

The prospect returns with a bottle of scotch.

He releases his hold on my cheek and instead holds out his hand. "Come on."

"Where are we going?"

"To get drunk."

"I'm more of a vodka girl." I indicate the scotch.

"Give it a couple of glasses," he tells me. "You'll change your mind."

I smile and slip my hand into his. He leads me through the clubhouse and up a set of stairs. It goes up for what feels like an eternity. I'm wheezing by the time we reach a door at the top. When he pushes through it, the cooler air hits me in a blast.

He steps out onto the roof of the building, still holding my hand. There are a few plastic white chairs positioned around a small table. He gestures for me to sit. Once I do, he takes the seat next to me.

The light pollution from the city makes it hard to see the dark ribbon of sky, but I can just about make out the little sparkling stars. There's some traffic moving around on the streets below, but the city is quieter than I've ever heard it.

Peace.

I feel it wrap around me.

It soothes me, makes the darkness abate a little. "It's beautiful up here."

"I love Manchester," he admits.

"Would you ever go back to London?" I ask. I hope the answer is no.

"It took a while to feel like home, but no… I don't think I could go back to London."

He hands me the scotch. I take a long sip of it, wincing at the burn and taste. "That's gross," I mutter, offering it back.

He drinks from the bottle too, smirking. "This shit is expensive."

"I'm a cheaper date," I tell him. Then cringe. Did I really just compare this to a date?

Howler doesn't seem to notice, or if he does he doesn't say. "Ain't nothin' about you is cheap," he says.

I want to believe that, but demons whisper untruths in my ear all the time. "I'm damaged goods," I disagree.

"You think that shit with the Jesters fucking defines who you are?"

I don't want to think it does, but how could it not?

"Howler… I was used like a toy. I have to wait months before I can have sex again in case those…animals gave me something."

It's the closest I've come to admitting what happened to me while I was captive. I hate the way it makes Howler's jaw tighten.

"They raped you."

The blunt way he says it makes me jolt. Fuck. It steals my breath from my lungs. I press a hand against my sternum as pain lances through my heart. I want to deny it, but I'm tired of pretending, of keeping it inside. I'm tired of putting on a mask for everyone to see. I'm breaking inside and I need to talk about it.

For some reason I trust Howler to listen.

"Yeah."

I glance over the city, letting my gaze unfocus on the lights below. It takes me a moment to realise the smear of colours I'm seeing is because I'm crying. I swipe angrily at my cheek. I don't want to shed any more tears for those monsters. They don't deserve it.

"The whole club?" Howler asks in a low, lethal sounding voice. "Or just that prick Wrecker?"

I give him my eyes, surprised by the anger rolling off him. He doesn't owe it to me to care. "Does it matter?"

"Yeah, babe, it matters. I need to know the punishment we dealt out was enough."

My heart twitches at that. It shouldn't warm me, but it does.

"Sometimes. Not all at once, though. Wrecker was the worst. And Griller."

He clamps his jaws together, his fingers interlacing behind his head as he struggles to compute the words.

"Knew it happened. It was fucking obvious, considering how we found you, but knowing and hearing it direct from your mouth...ain't the fucking same."

I want to soothe the pain rippling across his face, but I don't want to cross into his space. I get the impression he needs it. "I'm okay. I survived. Which is more than they can say." I try to lighten his rage with an attempt at brevity. It falls flat.

"Wish we could have tortured every fucking man in that club."

"Dead is dead, Howler," I say, keeping my voice soft. "Knowing they can't touch me is enough."

Apart from the Jesters' president. He's still out there, still breathing. I'm not a blood-thirsty person, but I want him to suffer the humiliation, the degradation I did. I want him to beg for mercy that Howler will never deliver.

"Wrecker is going to pay with more than his life."

I peer into the inky sky. "So now you know how damaged I am."

He shakes his head. "This shit ain't your burden or your shame to carry, Pia. I'm not a good man, don't profess to be one, but I'd never fucking harm a woman like that. None of my brothers would. They'd be stripped of their kuttes the moment they did."

"I think Wrecker saw it as a challenge to see who could hurt me the most."

I have no idea why I'm opening up to him, but I can't stop my mouth from moving. I risk glancing in his direction and the fire blazing in his eyes frightens me.

"Howler? Are you okay?"

"I'm trying to keep my temper under fucking control," he grinds out.

"I'm okay," I try to assure him.

"Except you ain't sleeping."

"I think nightmares are expected after something like that." I sigh, sinking back into the chair. "I'm not sure how

I'm supposed to go back to my normal life after this. How do I go back to life, like none of this happened?"

"I don't know."

I take the bottle back off him and take a swig, relishing the burn this time as it hits the back of my throat. "Not that I had a life. Max ripped that shit out of me long before the Jesters did."

"Why'd you stay with him?"

I shift my shoulders. "I thought it would get better."

"Pricks like that don't change."

"Yeah, I figured that out the hard way." My smile is wry. "Things weren't always bad with Max."

Howler snorts. "The man sounds like a fucking dick."

"He was towards the end, but it didn't start out like that."

"It never does," he says.

"I don't think Mum is going to let me out of her sight again."

"You can stay at the clubhouse as long as you want to."

"Why? I don't believe you're doing all this just because my mum and Socket dated twenty years ago."

"Valentina is important to my brother. That makes you important to the club."

I mull over his words, but something just doesn't make sense. I drink a little more, starting to feel pleasantly warm (and a little buzzed) from the booze. My head feels like it's starting to float and my muscles are loose.

"Your club is so different from the Jesters," I muse.

"Those fuckers aren't a club." The growled anger doesn't surprise me.

"I can see that. You lead your men and they follow because they respect you. Wrecker never had that from his brothers. He ruled through fear, mostly." A shiver works up my spine as his face dances across my memory.

I close my eyes briefly before taking another swig of the scotch.

"Wrecker's a weak fuck, but I'm as much to blame. I didn't see the Jesters as a threat," he admits. "I thought they were just weekend riders, playing at the big leagues. I wish I'd fucking chased them out of town when I was getting the Sons established. I fucked up."

I reach out, the booze making me bold, and grab his hand. His tattooed skin looks so warm compared to my paleness. "This isn't on you."

His gaze roams over our joined hands before he meets my eyes.

Something passes between us, a moment I can't explain. I'm hurtling forwards at a hundred miles per hour and he's got his arms out, ready to catch me. My breath tears out of me as he stares at me. He's not seeing pieces he needs to scrape up. He's seeing me.

Just me.

I want to kiss him.

The need is clawing at my skin like an itch I need to scratch.

I don't know where the fuck it comes from, but I need to have him.

I lean across in my chair and, without invitation, I press my mouth to his.

For a moment he doesn't respond. I start to pull back,

wondering if I've made a huge mistake. Embarrassment washes through me and my face feels hot in a way I know it's not the booze warming my cheeks.

He pulls back a little, his mouth close enough to mine that I can smell the scotch on his breath.

"Pia." He says my name in a desperate strangled tone. Does he not want this?

I start to pull back, feeling tears pricking my eyes. He said I'm not damaged, but the way he's looking at me now, the way he thinks this is too much too fast, tells me I am.

"Sorry," I mutter, turning away.

He lets me go for a second, then he grabs the back of my neck, forcing me back to him. A tingle of panic rolls through me, visions of Wrecker and his brothers flashing through my mind. They dissipate the moment Howler smashes his mouth against mine.

My toes curl in the thick bed-socks I'm wearing and I dig my nails into his biceps to ground me as he tangles his fist into my hair so he can deepen the kiss.

I don't know when it happens, but we're both out of our seats, arms wrapped around each other, kissing with a passion I've never experienced—even with Max.

It feels like touching heaven.

I'm floating on clouds as he continues to explore my mouth. I need more. I want more. While I'm kissing him, I'm not thinking about my rape, I'm not thinking about anything but how good Howler feels.

"The fuck?" a sharp voice demands from behind Howler.

Socket.

Howler is dragged off me and Socket surprises the hell out of me by slugging his president in the face. I cover my mouth, my eyes wide.

"Socket! Stop!" I yell.

Howler keeps his cool and holds his hands up as he takes a step back, as if that can keep the furious biker back.

The panic rolling through me sobers me up faster than anything else could.

"You fucking prick," Socket snarls. "She's off limits. To you, to every fucking man in this club!"

"Just calm down."

He might as well have thrown petrol on the flames. Socket roars.

"She isn't some skanky club whore you get to fuck and discard."

"We're not—"

"She's my fucking kid, you piece of shit!"

I'm not sure if he realises what he's said, but as he lunges for Howler, I feel as if I've been doused in ice.

The man standing in front of me, ready to defend my honour, is my fucking father?

Howler smashes his fist back into Socket's face, and now blood is pouring down both men's faces.

I get between them before another punch can be thrown, my heart hammering in my chest. I peer up at Socket, my eyes scanning his face, really studying the man who is claiming I share his DNA. Now that I'm looking at him, I see similarities between us. The same dark hair, the same slope to our noses. A familiarity that I didn't notice before. I stagger back. My brain refuses to believe what it is telling me. For two decades, I have lived fatherless. I'm not ready to embrace this new information.

"You're my father?"

He huffs out a breath and I can see the toll this is taking on him. "Yeah, kid. I'm your dad."

I stare at him a beat. Then I do the only thing I can. I slap him across the face hard enough to sting my palm.

CHAPTER 12
HOWLER

The sound of flesh meeting flesh sounds loud. If anyone else had raised a hand to Socket I would've had them on the floor, knee in their chest, knife to their throat.

But Pia isn't anyone.

She's his daughter.

And she deserves to be pissed.

They lied to her. For years.

I hang back, waiting to see what my brother will do. He absorbs the hit as if it is nothing, his head lowered.

I doubt this is how he intended for Pia to find out the truth. I doubt seeing me kissing his only child left anything but a bitter taste in his mouth, too. She'd been bold, brazen, even to instigate the kiss the way she had. It had shocked the fuck out of me, but if Socket hadn't interrupted us…

I don't know where things would have gone, but I'm pissed I didn't get to find out.

Pia's chest heaves as she stares at the man who gave her life. I can see the anger in every line of her body.

"Why?" she hisses out. "Why did you lie for so long?"

When his eyes find hers there is so much pain there, and not from the physical hit. This is deep rooted agony from knowing he's hurt his child.

"Pia…" The way he says her name, the feeling behind it, makes my chest cave in. Fuck. He's a man standing in front of his daughter begging her not to hate him.

The fire in her eyes suggests that's not going to be the case.

"Don't fucking Pia me. I've been here for weeks. You never once thought to mention you're my father?"

"It's been years. I didn't want to hurt you—"

"Yeah, because this is so much better. You and Mum… It was before you got locked up, right?"

"We were kids. I was looking at a long fucking time in jail. I didn't want you visiting me across a table."

"So you just pretended not to exist?" She paces away from him, one hand on her hip.

"I met your mother when I was fifteen. Loved her from the moment I laid eyes on her. Knew in that instant she was going to be mine."

"Then you left her to raise me alone. For twenty plus years."

He grimaces. "I made sure you were both taken care of."

"You weren't there. How would you know?"

"I kept tabs on you both. I sent Valentina money so she could raise you."

Pia's expression darkens. "I didn't need money. I needed my father."

Socket shakes his head. "I went to prison at nineteen, Pia. I got fifteen years inside. My life felt like it was over. You would have been nearly grown by the time I got out. When Valentina told me she was pregnant, I wanted with every bone in my body to be a dad—to be your dad—but I never wanted you in that place. I never wanted to dirty you with the shit I've done. So I let you go. I let you live your life without my filth touching you."

She glares at him. "That wasn't your decision to make."

"As your dad it was. I did what I thought was in your best interest."

Pia's gaze goes out over the club compound. She's barely keeping it together. If he pushes her she'll break down. I can see it in her eyes, the pain, the anguish of what she's learnt. "What did you do to get fifteen years?"

Socket tightens his jaw. "Doesn't matter."

"It matters to me."

"I..." He grimaces. "I killed a man."

Her eyes flare. "Why?"

"It doesn't matter."

She shoves him. "Don't do that. Don't baby me! I deserve to know why you threw our life away."

"Because he hurt your mum. The circumstances of what happened got me a lesser sentence, but it was still long enough."

Pia recoils back, her expression morphing into one of horror. "Hurt her how?" Has her mind gone to worst case scenarios, like what happened to her?

"It's water under the bridge, kid."

"Not to me it's not."

"It's not my story to tell."

Pia glances away and fuck, I wonder what the hell is going through her head. I shouldn't be here for this shit, but leaving her here isn't an option. I want to make sure she's okay.

Her gaze suddenly snaps to my face. "Did you know about this?"

Fuck.

"Yeah," I admit.

I watch the betrayal ripple across her face, my stomach clenching. I've never given a fuck about making a woman happy, but the look she's giving me hits my heart like a pick axe.

"So you all lied to me?"

"Ain't like that, Pia," I try to explain, but she holds a hand up.

"You didn't tell me and you knew. That makes you as bad as him and my mother." She shakes her head, as if she can't believe what is going on. I don't like the pain in my chest and I don't like the way she's breaking apart in front of my eyes. "I've been here for weeks. You could have told me the truth at any point. Instead you all lied."

"Pia—" Socket steps towards her.

"Stay fucking back," she hisses.

She storms back through the door into the clubhouse, slamming it behind her. For a moment the silence spans between me and Socket.

"She'll come around," Socket says.

Anger blazes through me. "You should have given her the truth weeks ago, when she first fucking got here."

Socket clenches his jaw. "Don't remember asking for your opinion on that."

Normally I wouldn't give it. It isn't my business what my brothers do, but I feel protective of Pia. Seeing her hurting fucking cuts through me. "You just made shit about a hundred times harder between you both. You think she's going to trust you now?"

I start to move past him, intending to go after her. Socket snags my bicep. "The fuck is going on between you two?"

"Don't remember asking for your opinion on that," I fire back at him.

"She's my daughter, Howler. Respect you, respect your position, but you don't get to use and discard her."

"That ain't what I'm doing," I assure him. It's not. I wasn't sure what I felt for Pia until this moment, but forced to face my feelings, I realise how much she does mean to me. I realise I'm willing to fight for her, too.

"She's been through fucking hell." He doesn't need to remind me of that fact. I know.

"Yeah, she has been."

"So she doesn't need you screwing with her fucking head by kissing her."

He makes it sound so base, so sordid.

"Whatever is going on between me and Pia ain't your business, Socket. She might be your kid, but she's a grown fucking adult who means something to me. I'm not going to fucking back off just because you feel like playing her dad." He clenches his fist at his side. "You throw that punch we're going to have problems," I warn him.

"She's my daughter," he repeats, but this time there's a pleading note in his voice.

"Ain't going to treat her like shit. Ain't going to make her do shit she ain't ready for either, but ain't walking away. Not because you ask it. She needs a friend."

"Friends don't fucking lock tongues, Howler."

"You need to decide what role you want to have in your daughter's life and fucking fight for it."

I move past him, irritation lacing every inch of my body. Does he really think I would take advantage of Pia after everything she has been through? I know my actions are enough to make him suspicious of my intentions, but I figured the fucker knew me better than that.

I make my way down the stairs to the ground floor. I don't need to figure out where Pia has gone. I can hear her.

I follow the yells into the common room and see her standing in front of her mother.

There are tears in Valentina's eyes as her daughter confronts her. "You have to understand, Pia, we did what we thought was best for you."

"Lying to me, leaving me without a father in my life—that was best for me?" Pia yells.

"At the time, yes. It was."

"It wasn't your choice to make! I had the right to know my father!"

"Pia—"

"Fuck you and fuck him."

She storms from the room. I meet Valentina's eyes, seeing the sadness there, then I go after Pia.

I find her in the garden, sitting on a bench. She's struggling to get a cigarette out of the packet. Slowly, I make my way over to her.

"No offence, but I don't want to talk to you, either," she mutters as she manages to get one free. She places it between her lips.

I pull out my lighter and click it down, the flame jumping to life. She glares at me before leaning into the flame.

When it's lit I return my lighter to my pocket and watch her as she takes a long drag.

"Does everyone know he's my dad? Everyone except me."

"Socket told us so we'd help retrieve you from the Jesters."

"That's why you came to get me. Because I'm Gavin's kid?"

"Yeah. You're club family. We would have rode into hell to get you, darlin'."

"Even though Gavin doesn't know me?"

"Yeah."

"You didn't think to mention it during one of our many conversations?" she asks.

"Wasn't my place, darlin'."

She offers me a cigarette. It's an olive branch, one I take. I sit next to her and light it. The first hit of nicotine is soothing as it hits my lungs.

"They did what they thought was best," I say. "They were barely more than kids themselves."

"I would have rather seen him in prison than not had a father at all. I grew up thinking my dad hated me and that's why he wasn't around."

"Socket might have been fucking misguided, Pia, but the minute Valentina asked for help he gave it. Without question. He does love you."

Her jaw goes solid as she glances down at her lap. "How am I supposed to reconcile this?"

"Depends what you want out of it."

"Meaning?"

"Do you want to know your father or not?" She doesn't answer. Maybe she doesn't know how to yet. "He did a shit thing," I continue. "You're right to be pissed. I would be too, but you also have a chance to get to know the man if you want to."

"I'm too mad to even think about it yet." She takes a long drag, blowing the smoke out a moment later. "If I hadn't been taken, would they ever have told me the truth?"

Probably not. I don't say that because we both know the answer.

She turns to face me. "Before this bombshell was dropped on me we...uh...we *kissed*."

"Yeah."

"I'm sorry."

"You didn't want to kiss me?"

"I didn't say that, but it puts you in a weird position. Especially now I know Gavin's my...dad." She stubs her smoke out, dropping the end into the ashtray next to the bench.

"I wasn't thinking about Socket, babe."

Her expression is filled with curiosity as she studies me. "What were you thinking?"

That I wanted her. More of her. Fuck, I should walk away and not be the bastard Socket thinks I am. She has been through hell, but I lean forwards and this time I make the first move.

I press my mouth to hers. She melts instantly against me, any sign of discomfort or unease nowhere to be seen. I want to devour her, to kiss her like I own her, but I'm aware she needs soft and careful from me, and I'm willing to give it. I'm willing to do anything she needs.

She moans against my lips as I lick inside her mouth, my tongue sliding over hers. I notice the little shivers that go through her body as I cup her neck, drawing her closer. I pull her lips between my teeth before I suck on the bottom one. Her eyes are closed as she kisses me back, her fingers digging into my biceps, as if she needs an anchor to ground her. I'm happy to be that. I'm happy to do whatever she needs.

I don't want to demand more than she can give, but my movements are desperate, needy. She's like kissing heaven.

When we break apart, we're both breathing heavily. I want to push her back on the bench and eat her pussy, but she isn't ready for it. She's still healing and I respect that.

She brushes her fingers over swollen lips. "Thank you," she says.

"For what?"

"For not treating me like glass that might break." Her fingers fist the edge of the bench. "Everyone is walking on eggshells around me."

"Everyone just wants to make sure you're okay, darlin'."

"It doesn't define me," she says in a strong voice. "It happened, but it's not going to be a part of my future too. I won't let it."

"You don't have to let it," I agree.

"I'm tired of being cooped up. I feel like a caged bird."

I don't blame her for feeling that way. She's been staring at the four walls of the clubhouse for weeks.

We need to be careful, but that doesn't mean she can't go somewhere with protection. I stand up and she peers up as I hold my hand out to her.

"You want to get out of here?" I ask when she doesn't move.

"And go where?"

"For a ride."

Her brow arches. "A ride on what?"

"My bike."

Her nose scrunches up.

"I don't know how to ride a motorcycle, Howler."

"I'll be riding, you'll be behind me."

If she understands the gravity of what it means to ride bitch, she doesn't show it. I follow her tongue as it dips out to wet her bottom lip. I can't stop from tracking the movement.

"It's safe to go?"

"I'll take care of you, darlin'," I assure her.

She considers this for a moment before she nods. "Okay."

She takes my hand and I pull her to her feet.

"You'll enjoy this, I promise."

CHAPTER 13
PIA

I wait at the bikes while Howler gathers a few other brothers to come with us. Warmth spreads through me that he wants to protect me. Wrecker is still out there and a very real threat. I know what the man is capable of. I've experienced it first hand, and while I would prefer it to just be the two of us, I feel better when he emerges with Trick and Terror, a helmet clutched in his hand.

Howler leads me over to a huge black and chrome Harley. He helps me put the helmet on, his fingers scraping over my chin as he fastens the strap. Then he reaches for the helmet sitting on the back of the bike, pulling that on his head.

"Okay, rules are simple: You lean when I lean, same direction or we'll come off the bike, you hold on tight the whole time. I don't have a bitch bar so you're going to have to hold on to me. Oh, and be careful not to touch the pipes. They get fucking hot. You ain't really dressed to ride, but I ain't crashed in over a decade and a half of riding. Ain't going to start with you on the back of my bike."

Terror and Trick exchange glances as Howler climbs on the motorcycle. I don't know what that look means, but my attention is captured as Howler turns to me.

"Get on behind me."

I use his shoulders to steady myself as I place a foot on the foot peg and swing my leg over the back. He's solid as a rock as I sit down. I notice how close this puts me to his back, my pussy practically squashed against him. "Um... how do I hold onto you?"

He grabs my hands and draws them around his waist. This draws me even closer. I'm sure my breath is lodged in my throat as he runs his fingers over my arms.

"Keep a good grip," he says.

Then he starts up the bike. It rumbles for a second before it comes to life, growling beneath us. The vibrations are powerful between my legs as he revs the throttle.

As the bike lurches forwards, I squeal and lean into his back, my grip around his waist tightening. The wind attacks my clothes as he directs the bike into traffic, Terror and Trick falling into formation behind us. I cling desperately to him, remembering what he said about leaning with him. After a time, the city fades away into the distance and the road winds through the hills of the Peak District National Park. I lift my head from where it's buried in Howler's back and take in the scenery. It's desolate, a wasteland of greenery, but it's beautiful and wild, too. The wind whips across my face as the bike twists and turns down the single carriage road that snakes through the landscape.

I close my eyes, enjoying the sensations rolling over me, and I realise for the first time in months I feel at peace.

There's no Wrecker. I'm not a victim. Socket isn't my father. My mother didn't lie to me, and I didn't kiss Howler.

There is just me and the open road.

It's freeing.

I feel alive.

My heart beats.

Lub-dub.

Strong and loud in my chest.

I turn into the wind. All I'm aware of is the man I'm clinging to. The man I kissed. The man I think could save me from drowning in the filth Wrecker and his brothers covered me in.

I bury my face in his kutte, smelling leather and his aftershave. It's a heady mix. He makes my head spin. I know I should be angry that he lied to me—that he didn't tell me who my father is—but I don't think there was any malice in it. Howler doesn't know me. He had a duty to Gavin to keep his secret. I'm not sure I can be angry at him for being a good friend, a good brother.

We turn on a road surrounded by large conifers. The bike races up the hill, taking the bends easily. I do as I was told and lean into each turn of the bike. It's easy to find that rhythm after a while, becoming one with the motorcycle.

After a time Howler starts to slow the bike. I glance over his shoulder as he pulls onto a small layby that looks out over the hills. As he rolls to a stop, his feet touch the ground, steadying the bike. He glances over his shoulder at me. "Jump off."

I use his shoulders to climb off the back of the bike, surprised by how much my legs tremble as I hit the ground. Trick and Terror are both kicking down their stands at the turnaround.

Adrenaline flows through my veins as I stand on solid ground again. "That... was..." I don't have the words to explain what it was.

Howler grins at me. "Yeah, babe, I get it." He undoes his helmet and rips it off his head, his hair flattened a little. It doesn't make him look any less attractive.

And Howler is attractive. He has this unattainable quality about him that is appealing.

"I understand why you ride. I've never felt so free."

He takes my hand in his and pulls me over to the small fence at the edge of the layby. He leans back against it, his elbows on top of the wood, his foot leaning against the bottom piece.

"This is one of my favourite places to come. If I need a moment to collect my thoughts, or to think about things, this is where I end up."

I move to the fence and stand next to him, facing out over the valley. I can understand why he would find solace here. Other than that occasional buzz of a car passing on the road behind us, it's quiet. I can hear sheep in the distance bleating, and the sound of maybe a tractor or some kind of farm machinery, though I can't see any houses nestled amongst the hillsides. "I think I'd need a lot of moments to collect my thoughts," I say on a breath. "The view is amazing." The fresh air soothes me in a way nothing else could. The imaginary shackles that were latched around my wrists in the clubhouse disappear.

"Yeah, it is." I glance up at Howler and realise he's not looking at the hills. His gaze is locked on my face. Heat fills my cheeks. He is talking about me. He takes my chin between his fingers and tilts my head so he can brush his lips against mine.

I lean into him, pressing against the length of his body as he continues to devour my mouth. I don't feel any fear with him. He is always so careful, mindful of my past trauma. I know he would never push me farther than I am able to go. I trust him, even though I barely know him.

The kiss is bold, without any hesitation or uncertainty. He takes what he wants and I allow it. Because I want him. I feel comfortable with him. I never thought I would feel comfortable with another biker again, not after what happened, but Howler has proven himself to me.

My arms tangle around his waist as his fingers come to rest on my neck. I feel like I'm floating, even as my heart pounds a staccato beat.

When he finally unlocks his lips from mine he's breathless. So am I. He cups my jaw as he rests his forehead to mine. "You're like a drug. I can't get enough of you."

Considering I feel the same, my stomach does a little flip-flop. "Kiss me again," I order.

He complies, dipping his head once more and taking my mouth. Unease ripples through me for a moment as Wrecker enters my mind. It's not Howler standing in front of me, lavishing affection on me. It's the nightmare that tails my every step. I jolt in Howler's arms, panic engulfing me. My body feels like it's been electrocuted. I'm short of breath, my heart starting to race in my chest as moisture covers my skin, making me sweaty and clammy at the same time. I want to stumble back, but he keeps his grip on my arm. "Okay?"

Embarrassment floods me. "I'm sorry."

He doesn't move towards me, but I can tell he wants to. "Don't do that. Don't apologise. You went through hell, Pia. That doesn't go away overnight. We don't have to do this."

My head snaps up, my eyes finding his. "I want to." I'm not scared of Howler or him hurting me, and I don't want him to think I am. I don't want to flinch when he touches me sometimes. I don't want Wrecker in my head when I'm with someone else, someone I care about.

He reaches out slowly, testing me, and cups my face. I don't flinch this time. "Cut yourself some slack," Howler says.

"He's in my head sometimes," I admit. "They all are, but Wrecker is the one I'm most…scared of."

"Mara can find someone for you to talk to—if you want to."

I don't, but I don't want to feel like this, either. I don't want that prick in my head when I'm with Howler.

"Okay," I agree.

He dips his head and kisses me. This time, Wrecker doesn't enter my thoughts and I just savour the moment with a man who is coming to mean everything to me. I shouldn't rely on him, but I can't help it. No one else has shown me such kindness.

When he finishes taking my mouth, he pulls back and trails his fingers over my cheek. "We need to get back."

I don't want to leave, but I nod. He leads me back over to the bike, ignoring the other two brothers with us and helps me get my helmet on. Then, together, the four of us hit the road back into Manchester city centre.

CHAPTER 14
HOWLER

As soon as I pull the bike into the clubhouse parking area, I spot Socket waiting for us. The way his mouth is fixed in a tight line tells me how pissed he is. I don't blame him for his anger. I took his kid out while there is a lunatic wanting revenge, but I didn't go out half-cocked. I took protection with us.

I stop the bike and wait for Pia to climb off. Then I kick down the stand and get off myself. Socket strides over and I can feel the anger pulsing off him.

"Are you fucking crazy?" he hisses.

"Careful," I warn. He might be Pia's father, but I'm still his president.

"That cunt Wrecker is still out there and you take my daughter out—on the back of your fucking bike!"

Having freed her head from the helmet, Pia rounds on him. "You don't get to play at my father now, Gavin. You had two decades to be that for me."

Socket recoils as if she struck him. Fuck, the last thing

I want is to come between him and her and their relationship—however that will look.

"Pia, why don't you go inside," I say, my eyes never leaving Socket's face.

"I don't need to go inside," she fires back. I give her my attention.

"Inside," I repeat.

She must see something on my face because she huffs and turns towards the clubhouse. I watch her until she's inside, then I turn to Socket.

"Know you want to protect her. Know you think I'm taking advantage, but I ain't doing any of that. I care about your daughter, Socket." I more than care about her, but I don't think now is the best time to drop that on him. "I wasn't going to let shit happen to her, but she needed to get out of the clubhouse. She was going crazy staring at the walls every day."

"That prick is out there, Prez. He is biding his time, waiting for the right moment to strike back at us. It isn't safe for her to be out there."

"Wrecker kept her a prisoner. For months. I wasn't about to do the same."

I can see my words affect him. He tears a hand through his hair. "Fuck. I just want her safe."

"So do I."

"I fucked up with her. She's never going to fucking forgive me for what I've done."

I don't want to give him false hope. His actions, however admirable at the time, have consequences. Pia should have been given the choice about whether she wanted to know her father in prison or not. Her parents stripped that away from her and that's why she's so angry. This isn't something Socket can fix in an afternoon. He's going to have to work hard to win his daughter over.

"Don't give up on her. She'll come around, but you have to prove to her that you're going to be here."

"Prez," Blackjack says as he jogs across the tarmac towards me and Socket. "One of my contacts has found the ex-husband."

Max. That slippery little cunt is going to die for what he's done. I'm going to torture the fuck out of him and when I'm done Socket will want to go at him, too.

"Let's go get the bastard," I say.

We don't take our bikes. We are too noticeable. Instead we take the club's van. We might need it anyway to bring Max back. I need him someplace private, where I can take my time with him. The only place to do that is behind the walls of our clubhouse.

Blackjack climbs into the front seat. Socket and I get into the passenger side. The bench is supposed to seat two people, but Socket and I are both big men, so it's a squeeze. I leave Trick and Terror behind with the rest of our brothers to protect our clubhouse. As my vice president navigates the streets of Manchester, my anger grows with each passing second. Max destroyed Pia's life, and I want to destroy his in return. Who fled and left his partner to pick up the pieces of the mess he'd created? I could never imagine doing that to someone I love. There is no excuse he can give me that will make me go easy on him. I want him to suffer.

We head south out of the city, towards Alderley Edge, an area that is home to the rich and famous. I don't like going this far outside of our own territory, but the likelihood of gangs existing in this wealthy suburb city is slim.

It's nearly twenty miles from the clubhouse and it takes us over forty minutes to get there with the traffic. The houses out here are bigger and bolder, with massive driveways and double electric gates at the front. I can smell the money in the air, can tell by the cars moving through the area.

Blackjack leads us deeper into the town and to a sprawling mansion on the outskirts. I grit my teeth as we pull up outside. This cunt was living in luxury while his wife was being tortured and raped. Socket's mind must go to the same place as mine, because he snarls under his breath and hisses out, "He's mine."

I know I should give this to him. Pia is his daughter, but all I can think about is exacting my own revenge. Socket isn't the one who sat with her while she tried to sleep. Socket isn't the one who had conversation after conversation with her, trying to get her to break down those walls and confess so she can heal. I did all of that. I feel responsible to ensure Max gets what he deserves. More than that, I want to do it myself.

Pia means something to me. The need to avenge the wrongs done to her burns through me savagely. They tried to destroy her—Max, Wrecker, the Jesters. It is a testament to what kind of person she is that she has remained strong.

Blackjack parks the car outside the house on the kerb

line. I'm already seething as he cuts the engine. I'm glad we chose to leave the bikes behind. We would have stuck out in this neighbourhood like a sore fucking thumb. No doubt some nosy curtain twitcher would have called the pigs.

Socket and I get out of the van and move towards the gates in front of the house. There is a large brick wall circling the property, but I can see the gate-opening mechanism on the other side. I move to the wall.

"Hoist me up," I say.

Socket joins me in front of the wall, lacing his fingers together to create a step. I put my foot on it and hoist myself up so I can catch the edge of the brick. With little effort I pull myself onto the wall and drop down the other side. I land in the grass, bending my knees to absorb the fall.

Pausing in front of the gate, I take a moment to work out how to open it. When I hit the button the gate creaks and start to swing inwards.

I wait for Socket to get back into the van and for Blackjack to drive it through the gates before I reclaim my seat in the front. The driveway is massive, a straight run to the house which sits at the end of it. It looks enormous, ground stop-red brickwork and sash windows are spread across the front of the structure and there is a large storm porch over the front door. Landscaped gardens and flower beds sit beneath the windows, perfectly manicured.

"Is this his place?" Socket growls.

"Ain't sure," Blackjack says. "Ain't in his name, but he

was easy enough to track with the paperwork. Makes me think Wrecker knew where he was and didn't care."

That statement inflames me. Wrecker didn't look for Max because he had what he wanted. Pia.

Blackjack stops the van near to the front door. The three of us pile out. I don't bother to knock; I just test the knob and find the door locked. Blackjack kneels on one knee and pulls out his lock-picking kit. I glance around, noting we are hidden from the road. It wouldn't bother me if we weren't, but I'd rather nobody interrupted us during this.

My VP has the door open in less than a minute. Locks are designed to make us feel safe, but there are very few that cannot be easily opened. They aren't a deterrent to criminals determined to get inside. Just a minor inconvenience.

Blackjacks twist the knob on the door, which swings open onto a magnificent hallway. I can see the money in every piece of furniture as we step inside the house. Gilded, framed mirrors, scrolled-leg tables, and artwork that doesn't look like cheap prints, but originals.

I growl under my breath as we move deeper into the house. We search the entire ground floor and find it empty. Did we come at a time when this prick is not home?

I glance out through the huge floor-to-ceiling windows at the pool. Crisp blue water refracts the light, creating shimmers. It's then I notice feet on a lounger facing away from us. I smack Socket in the chest and nod my head in the direction. As soon as he clocks what I'm seeing, his mouth pulls down.

The three of us move like predators, carefully pulling the patio door open a little so we're able to slip outside. The pool area is covered in a large glassed-in frame that makes the air sticky and hot, even though outside is cooler. The fucker hasn't heard us yet and as we get closer I realise it's because he has a pair of headphones in his ears and the tinny sound of music filters across the space.

Socket moves first, grabbing him by the throat and dragging him off the lounger. Max squeaks, like the little rat he is. "I have money," he pleads. What the fuck did Pia see in this guy? He's skinny as a rake, without a pick of meat on him. In his swim shorts he looks even smaller. There is an air of arrogance about him, as if he is a man used to getting everything his own way. I wonder if he broke down Pia piece by piece with his words over the years. I fist my hands at my sides, wanting to take them and smash them into his stupid smug face.

Socket pulls him closer, his knuckles whitening as he tightens his grip around his neck.

"Don't give a fuck about your money."

Max's eyes dart back and forth as he tries to figure out why we are here. Then it seems as if he notices the kuttes on our backs. The colour drains from his face. "Jesters."

"No, but you're going to wish Wrecker got hold of you first."

Socket drags him over to the pool and forces him onto his knees on the tiles, then he pushes his head under the water. Max thrashes as his head is submerged. I move to keep hold of his legs, stopping him from falling in. None of us wants this to be over too fast. Max is going to feel the same trauma Pia did. We're going to make him pay for every hurt he inflicted on her.

Socket drags him back up out of the water. Max sucks in a huge breath, spluttering. Water sprays everywhere and I smile. I hope it burns the back of his throat. I hope he feels like his lungs are burning with every inhalation. I hope he suffers.

"Stop!" he pleads.

I wonder if Pia begged when she was being raped. This fucker doesn't deserve any fucking mercy.

"Make me," Socket hisses before shoving his head back under the water. I watch, holding Max's legs tighter as he continues to thrash. Blackjack stands behind us, his arms crossed over his chest.

When Socket pulls him back up this time his face is pale, and he looks like he's struggling to breathe. I place a hand on my brother's shoulder, telling him to give him a break for a second.

Socket releases him with a shove, pushing him down onto the tile. On his knees, Max bends over, his palms pressed into the floor as he heaves in breaths. His dark hair drips into his face and as I stare at him I can't imagine how he ensnared a woman like Pia. She's smart, capable, feisty. This guy is like a wet rag.

"I don't know what I did to piss you off," Max says between sucking in breaths. "But I have money. I'll pay you whatever you want."

"Do we look like we need fucking money to you?" I

snarl at him. Max's eyes come to mine and I see the abject fear in them. Good, fucker; be scared.

He pushes his wet hair back from his face, staring between us. "Then what do you want?"

"You left my daughter to those monsters."

He slides his gaze towards Socket. "Your daughter?"

"Pia."

If possible, the cunt turns paler. "You're lying. She doesn't have a father. I mean of course she has father, but he's not in her life. She's never met him."

"You want to argue, boy?" Socket growls.

Max's eyes dart around, moving between me, Socket, and Blackjack. "She never mentioned her father was in a motorcycle club."

I move forward and grab him by the throat, dragging him to his feet. I get in his face, baring my teeth at him like a rabid dog. "How the fuck do you leave someone you love to deal with people like that? Do you have any idea what they did to her because of your mistake?"

He starts to tremble. "No, they would never have touched her. The mess was mine! They would have come after me!"

I think he genuinely believes that, it doesn't excuse what he did. He walked out on a woman he was supposed to love, until death do us part. Those were the vows he gave when he married Pia. "They did shit to her that you couldn't even imagine in your worst nightmares. So I'm going to do the same back to you."

CHAPTER 15
PIA

I'm sitting in the common room. Blackjack, my father, and Howler disappeared after we got back from riding. Gavin was pissed, which annoyed me. He's not been my father for two decades. Does he think he gets to swoop in now and play that role? What I do is none of his business, and as soon as he gets back I'm going to tell him that. He doesn't get to interfere in my life. He doesn't get to tell Howler how to behave around me, either. If he wants to kiss me, he can. That's not Gavin's business.

I glance up as Mum sits in the chair opposite me. This is taking a toll on her. There are big circles under her eyes, dark smudges that tell me she's not sleeping. She's usually so put together, but right now she looks like she's barely keeping it together. For that reason, I should go easy on her. But she facilitated these lies. She saw me every day of my whole life and never once mentioned my father was out there. "Can we talk?" she asks.

I shift my shoulders, not wanting to tell her the last

thing I want to do is speak to her. Mum sighs and glances up at the ceiling, as if asking for divine intervention. "I'm sorry."

That word stings more than it should. Does she think an apology can fix this? "You should have told me the truth. If you don't want him to be in my life, too bad. That's his prerogative. You should have told me he existed. That should have been my choice."

She reaches out and grabs my hand, as if she needs something to ground her. Maybe she just needs to be touching me, to stop me from pulling away. "They were his wishes. Would you have had me go against them?"

"You had a decision, Mum. You picked him."

She shakes her head vehemently. "No, I've always chosen you. I did what I thought was best for you. I didn't want you to know your father was out there and that he made a decision not to be in your life."

"It makes no difference. We can't change the past."

"No, we can't. But I do hope in time you will forgive him for what he did. We were young, foolish. He honestly thought it was best for you. He would never have done anything to hurt you, Pia. He loved you."

I push to my feet, irritation crawling up my skin like a thousand fire ants. "He loved me, just not enough to be my father."

I leave the common room and step out into the hallway beyond it. As soon as the door closes behind me I sag against the wall, leaning my head back. I don't know how to deal with any of this. How long am I supposed to hold onto my anger? Am I right to be angry? I have a chance to know my father, a chance I never thought I would have. I close my eyes and try to let calm wash through me. This is all too much for one person to handle. When I open my eyes again, something through the window at the end catches my attention. I see a van and a man being pulled out with a hood over his head. He's only wearing a pair of swim shorts, his bare chest exposed.

I know I should mind my business. That was the first rule of the Jesters. Hear nothing and see nothing. But my feet move before I can even consider my actions. As I push through the doors to the street outside the clubhouse, I see my father, Howler, and Blackjack heading through a side gate. I follow after them, and as I push through the gate, Howler is waiting on the other side, leaning against the wall. His motorcycle boot is pushed against the bricks. He glances up as I stop in my tracks and huffs out a breath. "You lost?" he asks in a dry tone.

"Who's that man? The one in the hood?"

He's going to lie to me. I've never known a biker tell the truth. So he surprises the hell out of me when he answers. "That was Max."

My eyes narrow. "Max, as in my ex-husband Max?"

He pulls out a cigarette and lights it, before offering me one. I shake my head, more focused on the fact he said Max is here. "We got word today where he was hiding out. We went, found him, brought him here."

"You found my ex-husband?" I don't know if the Jesters looked for him when I was with them, but Wrecker never mentioned getting close to finding Max. "How? Are you going to hurt him?"

Howler blows out a puff of smoke. "The cunt was living it up in a fucking mansion while you were being abused. Don't feel fucking sorry for him. He didn't give a shit about you."

I knew Max ran, leaving me to deal with the fallout of his mistakes, but hearing he was living it up in some mansion makes my stomach twist. I let out a dry laugh, devoid of humour. "That bastard."

"Your dad and I are going to make sure he pays for what he did."

Hearing him say my dad so nonchalantly makes me jolt. Gavin is my father. It's a statement of fact, but he threw it out there like it was nothing. "Don't call him that."

Howler doesn't apologise, not that I expect him to. I get the impression Howler is a man who doesn't apologise for a lot. "What do you want me to call him?"

"I don't know. This is a lot to get my head around."

Howler reaches out, his hand resting on my neck. I managed not to flinch at his touch: progress. Instead, I meet his heavy gaze, wondering what he's thinking. "No one is saying you have to have all the answers. But he is your father, and while that is the case, my club will do everything in its power to protect you. Including bringing slimy Max in."

"What are you going to do to him?"

"We're going to show him what happens when he crosses our family." A shiver runs through me at the strength of his words. He genuinely means it, and I wonder what lengths he would go to in order to protect those he considers family. I have to admit, it makes me feel secure in a way I never have. Growing up, it was just me and Mum. I never had any safety net, any family to fall back on.

"I want to speak to him."

Howler's expression doesn't give anything away. "No."

His refusal infuriates me. "It was me he wronged, not you, not Gavin. I want to talk to him."

"Understand that, even accept the reasons why, but you've been through so much already—"

I interrupt him before he can get started on that argument. "You don't get to decide what is too much for me. I want to get answers from him, and you're not going to stop me."

I start to walk around him and he reaches out, grabbing my wrist. "I'm just trying to take care of you."

I turn back to him and place my hands on his shoulders, then roll to my toes and press my mouth to his. Instantly, his arms wrap around my back, pulling me closer. I kiss him in a way that tells him without words what I'm feeling. I need him, but I need this more.

"I know, but I need you to also help me process this. I need this time with Max. I need to understand why he did what he did."

He leans his forehead against mine and I can see the indecision warring on his face. "Okay."

He takes my hand and I'm buoyed by his touch. He gives me the strength to walk into the building at the back of the clubhouse. I noticed the huge padlock, hanging loosely from the catch. Howler gives me a quick glance before he pushes the handle down and shoves the door open.

I step into the building, a room really. The floor is concrete, sloped down towards a drain in the centre of it. The walls are plastic-panelled; easy to wipe. I don't miss the hook hanging from the ceiling, or the bare bulb that gives out too much light, though not enough to chase the shadows from the corners of the room.

They have Max tied to a chair, his head lowered to his chest as his breath rips out of him. Gavin and Blackjack both glance in my direction. My father's eyes flare wide as soon as they lock onto me. Before he can go off on Howler, I speak. "I have the right to be here."

Gavin's mouth pulls into a sneer, but he steps back and gives me the space to move towards the chair. My mouth is suddenly dry and I lick my lips, trying to gain some moisture. I dreamt a hundred times of the things I would say to my ex-husband if I ever came into contact with him again. Most were angry ramblings, hatred for what he'd done, but as I stand in front of him I feel nothing but pity.

I go down to my haunches, balancing on the balls of my feet. "Max," I say in a quiet voice that has him jerking his head up. For a moment I can see the confusion, the disbelief that I'm actually stood in front of him.

"Pia."

I glance down at the ropes binding his hands to the arms of the chair before I bring my attention back to his face. He has a large lump on his forehead, but other than that he looks unharmed. "Why?"

His mouth works, opening and closing, as he tries to find the words for why he left me in the hands of demons. As I look at him I realise how weak and pathetic he is. I always thought he was strong, that he could do anything. I loved him, but as I look at him now all I feel is loathing. There is none of the excitement that used to stir in my belly when he was close. I feel disgusted by him. "I–I had no choice."

"You had a choice, and you made it. You walked away and you left me to face those animals, knowing what they were capable of." I laugh darkly, the sound so unlike me I barely recognise it as my own. "Do you know what they did to me? Do you know how they tried to break me?"

Tears brim in his eyes. It pisses me off. I ball my fist up and I slam it into his stomach. He lets out an *oof* and tries to lean forward as much as the ropes will allow him. I hit him again. It doesn't come close to the torment I suffered, but it does release some of the pent-up rage building inside me. "They beat me daily. They used me like I was their toy. Raping me over and over until I forgot who I was. You left me there." I beat my hands against his chest, driven now by nothing more than my emotions. "You were supposed to love me, Max. You were supposed to protect me!"

I fall backwards onto my bum and draw my knees up to my chest, letting my tears flow freely. I hear him swallow and his breath as it hacks out of him. "I didn't know. I didn't know they would do that."

I lift my head from my knees and glare at him. "They

are a motorcycle club that you stole a shit ton of money from. What did you think they were going to do?"

The helplessness on his face only fuels my anger more. He doesn't get to play the victim in this. "I thought they would come after me. I didn't think for a second they would hurt you, darling."

It's the wrong thing to say. I lurch at him and punch him in the face. My knuckles burn instantly, but I don't care. I'm in too much pain as it is to acknowledge it.

"Call me darling again and I'll rip your fucking bollocks off."

He ducks his head, closing his eyes. "I never meant for this to happen. You have to believe that. I love you—"

He flinches as I raise my hand, but I don't let it fall. "You can't love me. If you did, this would never have happened. Why did you even take their money? It's not like we needed it."

I see a flash of anger cross his face. "How do you think we had the lifestyle we had? The manicures, the champagne fucking breakfasts, the spa days, the new cars, the holidays in the fucking Algarve. How do you think we afforded that shit?"

I have no idea, because he never let me near the money. He never once hinted that we didn't have it, either. "Do you honestly think I gave a shit about that stuff? I would have been happy living in a fucking shed with you."

"Pia." I get to my feet and give him my back, I can never forgive him for what he has done.

"We are done. As soon as I can get myself sorted with a solicitor, we're getting a divorce."

"I don't want to get a divorce."

I round on him. "The days of me giving a shit what you want are long gone. You will give me a divorce and you will stay the hell away from me."

I rush for the door and slam through it. As soon as I hit the fresh air, I gulp it down like I've been starved of oxygen. I lean a hand against the wall to steady myself. How can he sit there and blame me for what happened? I feel a hand on my back and I jolt up until I realise it is Howler.

"Okay?"

I'm not, so I shake my head. He pulls me into his arms and hugs me close. I cling to his kutte, burying my head in his chest. "There were like a hundred things I wanted to say to him." My voice breaks as I speak.

"You need more time with him, it's yours."

I shake my head. "He's already had enough of me. I won't give him anything else." I pull back and peer up into his face. He brushes my hair back behind my ear, and I realise in this moment how in love with him I am. Everything about this man is dark, except the way he looks at me. He makes me truly believe in second chances. "Just... Let him go. I don't want you to torture him because of me. He'd never withstand it anyway. The man is a coward."

"Your dad isn't going to like that. He needs to feel like he's protected his daughter."

"He saved me. He protected me enough doing that."

Howler kisses me, making all my bad thoughts disappear. When he pulls back, I trail my fingers through his beard. "Max is the past. I want you to be my future."

It's a bold statement to make, and I hold my breath as I wait for him to answer me. "I'm right here, baby."

CHAPTER 16
HOWLER

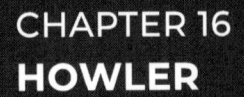

Pia heads back inside the clubhouse and I go back into the shed. Socket glances at me and I can see he's annoyed. "She okay?"

"Why don't you go and see and I'll take care of our little problem here?" He looks torn for a moment, wanting to dish out his version of vengeance on the man who caused his daughter so much turmoil, but wanting to comfort Pia, too. "She needs you. Go and be her father."

Socket relents and heads out of the shed, leaving me and Blackjack alone with Max. Pia didn't want him hurt, and as much as I want to keep that promise, I don't think I can. This cunt knew exactly what he was doing. You don't rob from an MC and expect to get away without any repercussions.

I pace the floor in front of Max's chair, enjoying the way his breath falters with each step I take. After a moment I stop in front of him and wrap my fingers around his throat. "Pia thinks I should go easy on you."

Relief shines in his eyes. "She's always been a good girl."

"I don't fucking agree with her." Panic flashes across his face and I relish it.

"I didn't know they would do that to her. I didn't know they would take her. The debt was mine, not hers. Why would they come for her?"

Blackjack steps forwards, a knife in his hand. "I don't believe you're that much of a dumb cunt, that you thought they would leave your wife alone."

I don't either. He served her up like a sacrificial fucking lamb. The whole time she was with them, being tortured and tormented, he was living the life of luxury in that fucking mansion. I squeeze his throat harder, watching his eyes bug in his head as he struggles to get air past my grip. "You left her to rot. You knew exactly what you were doing, and how to disappear."

His eyes are starting to get heavy, so I release my hold on his throat. He drags a breath in, tears running down his cheeks as he gasps for air. "I didn't know," he maintains breathlessly.

"I don't care if you knew or not. Your actions have consequences. Those fuckers raped her constantly, and when they weren't raping her they were beating her. While you breathed free, every day was a nightmare for her." I turn to Blackjack and take the knife from him. "And for that, you're going to pay."

I drag the knife down his chest, watching the blood bubble from beneath the blade. It goes some way to soothing the anger burning through me, but it's not enough. It will never be enough.

He screams like a prissy little bitch. I cut him again, then I glance at Blackjack, who shrugs at me. This is going to be over quick. I just want to put the fear of the fucking devil into him. I want him to leave Pia alone, give her the divorce she asked for and fucking disappear.

I hit him in the face, once, twice. He starts to cry. I've never brought a man into this room and had him cry before. How the fuck he thought he was going to take on the Jesters, I don't know. Wrecker is a cowardly piece of shit, but if he'd caught Max he would have done worse to him than we are.

I lean on the arm of the chair, trapping his arm between the wood and my hands. He tries to pull back, but there's nowhere for him to go. I get in his face. "You are going to give Pia the divorce she wants. You're going to sell that fucking monstrosity of a house you bought and you're going to give her the fucking money. And then you're going to leave her the fuck alone. You come near her and I'll cut your fucking balls off."

Max nods. "I'll do whatever. Just don't hurt me."

I straighten and crack my knuckles. "Oh pal, we are just getting started."

I beat the shit out of him, until his eyes are swollen and black. When I get tired, Blackjack takes over. It can't fix what was done to Pia, but it does make me feel some sense of righteousness.

Nursing bloody knuckles, I leave Blackjack to remove Max from the clubhouse and I go to find Pia.

When I enter the common room, she is sitting with Socket and Valentina. They look like they're deep in conversation and I don't want to intrude, so I make my way to the bar instead. Terror is sitting with Brewer and both brothers look up as I sit down. Terror's gaze goes to my busted-up knuckles and a smirk covers his face. "It's not fair that you got to have all the fun," he complains.

I shift my shoulders. "We still have to find Wrecker."

Terror cracks his knuckles and tilts his head from side to side, crunching his neck. "I can't wait to have a go with that slimy little cunt."

"You and me both, brother," I say before I glance around to where Pia is sitting. She doesn't look distressed, but she does seem to be annoyed. "How long have they been talking?"

"About an hour. There was some shouting to start with, but things have calmed down. Your girl's a firecracker."

Your girl.

It's the first time someone has acknowledged what Pia means to me. It doesn't scare me. I have no questions about claiming her as mine, but I'm not sure she's ready to take that step yet, and I don't want to push her further than she can go. On some level I knew she was mine the moment I laid eyes on her.

"Yeah, she fucking is."

The prospect brings me over a drink and some ice wrapped in a tea towel. I press it to my knuckles, wincing slightly at the pain. I don't regret rearranging that fucker's face for a moment, and it's not the first time I've had bruised or broken knuckles.

"We need to find Wrecker. The fact he has raised his head above whatever rat hole he's hiding in puts me on fucking edge." What the fuck is he planning? And why hasn't he struck back yet? We annihilated his entire club and burnt his clubhouse to the ground with the bodies of his brothers inside. If I were in his position, I would be building a fucking army to retaliate. The radio silence freaks me out.

Brewer shifts his shoulders. "Some cunts just be fucking cowards."

He's not wrong about that. Wrecker is a man who takes the wife of the crook who stole from him. He is the man who flees while his entire club is wiped out. He's a filthy, dirty little rat and I'm going to flush him out of whatever hole he's hiding in.

As much as I don't want to involve other chapters of the sons, I push up from my stool and make my way into the corridor outside. I call Ravage first, then I call Birmingham chapter's vice president, Grub.

My brothers get to work immediately, putting out feelers, trying to see if that slippery fuck is still even in the city.

By the time I return back to the common room, Pia is gone. I head out to the garden to see if she is there, but there are just a couple of brothers smoking. I go back inside and climb the stairs to the room she has been given while she has been staying with us. I've never knocked on a door in my life, but I find myself pausing before it. I wrap my knuckles of the wood and wait, like some kind of fucking dickhead, for her to open the door.

As soon as she does, I realise I was right to wait. She's in a pair of sleep shorts and a vest that hugs her tits in a way that should be fucking illegal for anyone else to see. I step into her space, forcing her to move back into the room. I shut the door behind us and turn back to her. Fuck, I want to be inside her so badly, but I won't risk throwing her off the edge that she's straddling. Pia might put a brave face on things, but I know she's struggling.

She looks relieved it's me in the doorway, and I wonder if she was expecting it to be her father, or her mother. Her eyes lower to my bloody knuckles before coming back to my face. "Is Max still breathing?" she asks.

"He's going to give you your divorce."

She cocks a brow. "That wasn't what I asked."

I scowl. "Yeah, I left that prick breathing, which is a lot more than he fucking deserves."

She goes to the bed and sits on it, pulling a pillow into her lap. "I know he did me wrong. I don't even understand why I wanted you to spare him."

I move to the bed, sinking down next to her. "Because you're a good fucking woman."

She ducks her head, shaking it as she does. "I don't think someone good would have all this bad happen to them."

I lift her chin with my finger. "Ain't your fault how other fuckers act. None of what happened is your fault, either, so get that shit out of your head."

She blinks away tears, but one falls, I swipe at it with

my thumb, wiping it off her cheek. I move onto the bed, sitting next to her, my back to the headboard, and then I pull her into my arms. She nestles against my side, her arm wrapping around my waist, and I can feel the tension leaching out of her as she does. "I just want to feel normal again." The whispered words cut through me like a knife.

"You are fucking normal."

She peers up on me, lifting her head off my chest. "Kiss me." It's not an order, but a plea.

I dip my head and do as she asks, capturing her mouth with mine. She melts against me, relaxing and putting all her trust in me. That makes me feel like Super-fucking-man. After everything she's been through, she trusts me to protect her and keep her safe. It's the best fucking gift she could give me.

She moves to straddle me, and I let her lead this, not sure where her head is at and not sure how far she wants to go. She pushes my kutte off my shoulders, and it is only then that I grab her wrist to stop her. "You don't have to do this."

"I want to." She reaches for my kutte again and this time I sit forward so she can get it fully off. I tug my T-shirt over my head, leaving me sitting bare-chested. She reaches for her vest top and pulls it off in one motion, revealing a plain black bra beneath. It's not fancy or lacy, but it is the sexiest fucking thing I've ever seen. I want to reach out and touch her, but I don't want to push. I glance up at her, waiting for instruction. "Babe, maybe we should just take a breath here."

Her face crumples and she starts to climb off me, muttering, "If you find me that disgusting just say so."

I grab her wrists, forcing her to stay in position. "Ain't said that, and you know it. I feel shit for you, more than I've ever felt for anyone, I don't want to push you into a place that you're not ready to go yet. It hasn't been that long. You need time to recover."

Her face contorts into an angry sneer. "Since it didn't happen to you, you don't get to tell me what I need."

Fuck. "You're right, ain't up to me to tell you how you feel."

Some of the anger fades from her. "I'm scared I'm never going to be able to do it again."

"Do what?"

"Have sex." She lifts off me and sits next to me, letting her head fall back against the headboard. "What if they broke me? What if I can never let anybody into my bed again? I want us to have something normal, Howler. I want to be able to make love to my man."

"Is that what I am? Your man?"

"I mean… I don't…"

I lean over and kiss her, saving her from having to answer. "You're mine, too."

She launches herself at me, and our lips crash together. I go down onto my back, bringing her on top of me. My hands skim up her bare skin towards her bra, and in one movement I unhook it, freeing her from it. She sits up slightly, giving me a tantalising view of dusky-pink nipples. I take one into my mouth, swirling my tongue around the bud as it starts to harden under my touch. She starts to pant, so I move my hand to cup her pussy. As soon as I touch her I know I've made a mistake. She screams and darts back. Her breathing tears out of her throat, followed by heavy pants as she puts the bed between us. I sit up, my heart beating in my chest like it has never beat before. She tears her fingers through her hair, her eyes darting around frantically. "I'm sorry. I'm sorry." I lean down and grab her vest, then I hand it to her.

"Ain't got nothing to apologise for. I can leave." I start to move off the bed.

"I don't want you to leave. I want to be able to be touched by somebody I'm pretty sure I'm in love with." She sobs out the words, so it takes me a moment to realise what she's actually said.

I pull my tee on, leaving my kutte off, and then I sit back on the bed and gesture for her to sit with me. "Ain't no rush for that. Ain't expecting it, and I don't want it if you're not ready."

She crawls next me, leaning her head against my chest once again. "What if I'm never ready?"

I kiss her head. "You will be, but you have to do it at your own pace, not at the pace you think I want to go at." For a moment we both sit in silence, my fingers stroking over her. Then I say, "And I'm pretty sure I'm in love with you, too."

CHAPTER 17
PIA

Lying in Howler's arms feels right. I'm embarrassed I freaked out, but he hasn't made it awkward or uncomfortable. If anything, he has been a beacon of strength for me. When I'm with him I feel invincible, like I could do anything. Like I can get over anything. He traces patterns on my arm as I lay plastered against him.

"How did you come to be with the club?" I ask.

"I used to run with the London chapter. Prospected for them, earned my colours, even got a seat at the officers' table. Ravage wanted to expand our club. At that point we had London and Birmingham. Manchester had gone through a transition. Gang warfare was rife. Guns were everywhere. Drugs, too. There was a lot of money to be made." He moves his hand to my hip, pulling me closer against him. "We knew we could slice out our own little corner. He asked me to come and I jumped at the challenge."

"How long have you been here for?"

"Seven or eight years. I forget exactly. My time with the London chapter seems a lifetime ago. This is home now. Blood was spilt to create our own little paradise and I'll bleed to keep it."

Images of bloody fighting cross my mind, and I wonder how much danger he was in while he was trying to create this so-called paradise. It makes me shiver, contemplating the fact he might have come close to losing his life.

"And the danger has passed now?"

"There are always new gangs setting up shop. We take them down fast before they can get rooted into the city, but there's only so much we can do. We protect our patch —nothing beyond it. We've earned a name for ourselves, though, and most of the other gangs and clubs avoid us." He kisses the side of my head and I can't help from leaning into it. "You're safe. You're family, part of this club, and that keeps you protected. Anyone who touches you knows they will have the full wrath of the Sons."

I peer up at him. "If the Jesters had known Socket was my father, would they have left me alone?" As soon as I ask it I wish I could take back the words, but I also want to know. Did my father's denial of me put me in danger that could have otherwise been avoided? The thought makes my gut churn.

His fingers still for a second before he resumes stroking me. "I don't know. Wrecker is reckless. Even our name might not have kept him from you if he wanted you enough."

As always, the mention of his name makes me shudder. "What is your real name?"

I don't expect him to answer. These men are attached to their road names. "Jacob Ryland, growing up everyone called me Jake. I fucking hate Jacob."

"Jake." I test the name on my tongue, liking how it sounds. Howler clearly does too, because he leans over and presses his mouth to mine. This kiss is warm, soft, but possessive. When he pulls back I smile at him. "How did you end up as Howler?"

He smirks. "Babe, ain't telling you that story."

I sit up slightly and look at him. "Why not? Is it embarrassing?"

"It was just drunken stupid shit that came about when I was newly patched in."

"Well, now you have to tell me, I'm completely intrigued!"

"I'm in bed with the most beautiful fucking woman I've ever laid eyes on. You think I want to talk about my fucking past?" He pulls me back on top of him and covers my mouth with his. His hands slide under my tee, resting on my lower back. I moan against him.

"That sounds like avoidance," I murmur against his lips as he slides his tongue along mine.

"The name ain't important."

"So then you won't mind telling me, will you?" I raise a challenging brow.

He forces out a breath, irritation lining the gesture. "Babe," is all he says. He doesn't need to say more, because his tone says everything.

I hold my hand up in defeat. "Fine! I can take a hint. You will tell me one day, though."

I snuggle deeper against his chest. For a while we just lie in silence, enjoying each other's company. His steady breathing is reassuring to me as I trace lines over the tattoos covering his chest. "I want to know my dad," I say.

"So get to know him."

"It's not that simple."

"Babe, the way I see it, life is not fucking guaranteed. We could both die tomorrow. You really want to have regrets?"

"That's morbid." I wrinkle my nose, not wanting to think about death.

"This life ain't the safest. Socket puts himself in the line of fire daily. Ain't nothing promised, especially not tomorrow."

His words make sense, even if I don't want them to. "I'm still mad at him. And my mum. They lied to me for years."

"They did."

"I'm not sure I can forgive that."

"I get that, and you have to come around yourself. Just... Don't take too long."

His phone buzzes on the bedside table and he leans over to grab it. I don't know what it says on the screen, but he mutters a curse under his breath. "I've got to go."

I want to whine, ask him to stay, but this is his life. He is president of a motorcycle club and that comes with responsibilities. How can I ask him to turn his back on everything he's built, just to spend time with me? "Okay," I say nestling back against the pillows as he extricates himself from under me.

"Okay?" He says as he pulls on his kutte, settling it in place.

I shift my shoulders. "Would you prefer I ranted and raved about you having to leave?"

He shakes his head and mutters a "fuck" under his breath. He moves over to the bed and dips low to kiss me. "Talk to your pops."

I ignore him and nestle further into the bed. I'm not sure I'm ready to forgive and forget. I'm not sure I'll ever be ready to do either.

He leaves the room and the silence closes in around me, letting my thoughts run rampant. Every time I close my eyes I see Wrecker and Griller. I can feel their hands holding me down as Boulder takes me. I know it's not real. I know I'm no longer there, but it feels so intense it lodges my breath in my chest. I sit up in the bed, rubbing at my sternum in an attempt to dispel the pain there. I swing my legs out and grab a clean pair of jogging bottoms from the drawers. Pulling them on, I find my bra and slip that on under my T-shirt. Then I head downstairs.

As always, the common room is filled with brothers and club bunnies. At first, I was horrified they kept these women here, too. But I've come to realise the sons treat their women with respect the Jesters never showed. I can't imagine a single one of these men ever forcing one of the women to do something they didn't want to. Even if they did, I can't imagine Jake putting up with it. I smile as I think of his name. He's been Howler in my head for so long his name feels borrowed, but I like the intimacy of being the only person who uses it.

Jake.

It suits him. I don't see Jake in the room, but I do see Gavin. He's sitting with Mum, their hands interlaced on the table. As I approach, they pull their hands away as if they have been burnt. Guilt pours through me. I think on some level, they really do love each other still. I don't want them to be something they're not, or pretend they don't care for each other because they're scared of upsetting me.

I sit down and I place their hands back together. "You still love each other," I say unnecessarily. It's obvious they do.

They exchange looks, like naughty teenagers caught in the act. "Yeah, darlin', I still love your mum."

The look on her face takes me aback. It's the first time I've ever seen my mum truly happy. It always seemed like there was something missing in her life, even growing up. Now, I know what that something was. It was Gavin. It was my father. All that time wasted, all that time they could have been together in some way or another. She could have visited him in prison. She could have been there when he got out. They could have found a way for us to be a family. That is what I find hard to forgive. They took that from me. The chance to have parents who loved me. I always thought my father didn't care, but that wasn't the case. In his own way, he did care.

"You shouldn't have lied. I had the right to know who I

was and where I came from. I had the right to know my father and that wasn't your decision to make."

"You're right." Gavin rubs a hand over his grey-streaked beard. "We fucked up, kid. I wish we could go back and change things, I wish… I wish…" He breaks off, closing his eyes, the pain on his face making my heart ache.

Without thinking, I reach out and I take his hand in mine. His eyes pop open and he peers down at our joined hands. "I understand why you did what you did. I don't agree with it, but I do understand. You were both young, and scared. You did what you thought was best. It's going to take me time to come to terms with everything, but I'd like to try and be a family."

Gavin lets out a breath that seems part relieved and part tired. "I want that more than anything, Pia."

"I'm not saying things are going to magically fix themselves overnight. That's not going to happen. I need time to get my head around everything, but I'd like to try."

"That's all I ask."

When I glance at my mum, I see she has tears standing in her eyes. Is this what she wanted all along? For us to be a family.

I excuse myself from them both and walk out to the garden. I sink onto a bench and pull out a cigarette, lighting it up. It's a habit I need to break, but for now it's the only thing that calms my nerves. As soon as that first hit of nicotine reaches my body, I feel the tension leach out of me.

I tip my head back to look at the sky, watching the

clouds move across the sea of blue. I don't feel at peace, but this is probably as close to that as I'm going to get. I take another drag before blowing out the smoke.

Something happening inside catches my attention. I turn on the bench so I can peer back through the windows of the common room. All I can see is men on their feet, and a raucous noise erupts. I stab my cigarette out, dropping it into the ashtray at the side of the bench and I rush inside.

The gathering crowd makes it difficult to see what is being focused on, but as I push past Trick and Blackjack I stop in my tracks. Kneeling in the middle of the floor is my nightmare. Wrecker.

His hands bound behind his back, his white T-shirt bloodied, and there's no sign of his kutte. His head is bowed, his head dripping blood into his face as the brothers step forward to kick him and jeer at him. Jake is standing behind him, his arms crossed over his chest, a triumphant smirk on his face.

Wrecker raises his head, as if he senses my presence. Fear clutches me and my stomach churns violently. A thousand memories collide in my mind. It takes everything I have not collapse. My skin feels prickly, too hot and yet cold at the same time. As soon as his eyes meet mine, I stumble back, hitting a hard wall of muscle. I glance up, fear clutching my chest, and realise I've backed into my father. His eyes are soft as he takes me in before he raises his stare to the man who destroyed me.

"Pia." That voice, my name on Wrecker's lips, nearly pushes me over the edge. He says it like poison, a smirk on his face as if he knows he can torment me just by speaking.

Gavin pushes me aside and grabs Wrecker by the front of his shirt. He drags him to his feet, bringing him an inch from his face. I can see the anger radiating off him in thick waves. "You're going to die, you piece of shit."

He meets Gavin's eyes defiantly before his gaze moves past him and locks on me again. I press a hand to my chest as my heart threatens to erupt through my sternum. "I've missed you."

CHAPTER 18
HOWLER

As soon as that cunt speaks to Pia, Socket rams his fist into his gut. Wrecker doubles over, gasping for breath. My eyes drift towards Pia. Her eyes are wide, her face pale as she takes in what's going on. Delivering him to her in this way might have been a mistake, but I was so caught up in the moment I didn't stop to think what it might do to her. Valentina has sidled up next to her and is holding her hand.

"Where did you find this fucker?" Socket demands. "Why the fuck wasn't I involved in bringing him in?"

I meet his glare. I understand why he would be pissed, but the call Blackjack made to me didn't leave a lot of time to rally the troops. One of our allies, a gang that has territory in Moss Side caught up with him and were holding him. They gave us an hour to collect him. I didn't think; I just got in the van with Blackjack and we drove across the city. I'm not sure what I expected when we got there, but this fucker tied up and ready for us to take was not it. I paid the fifty grand bounty we'd put on his head and we brought him back to the clubhouse. The whole drive back, all I could think about was what I was going to do with him. He's going to die for what he did; that's not in question, but how he dies... That's going to depend on a lot of factors.

As my gaze goes back to where Pia is standing, I see her turn and push back through the crowd. I follow after her immediately, and as I pass Blackjack I say, "Take him to the shed."

I rush out into the garden just in time to see Pia sink onto the edge of the bench. Fuck.

I go to her, crouching down in front of her. Her eyes raise to mine and I see the tears standing in them. "We got him."

"How?"

"Friend of a friend picked him up. Called as soon as they did."

"That's why you rushed out this morning?"

"Yeah. Didn't want to tell you in case it didn't pan out. Babe, if you want five minutes with him, you've got it."

She turns her head, her gaze going distant, as if she's looking but seeing nothing. "I-I can't." She closes her eyes. "I know that makes me weak, but being in the same space as him again... I just can't. I don't want to be—" She dissolves into sobs and I pull her off the bench, cradling her head against my chest.

"You don't have to do shit. We got this."

"What are you going to do to him?"

I lick my lips. I don't want to tell her the dirty filthy

truth of what we're going to do to him, but I want her to feel vindicated, like he got what he deserved for what he did to her. "You really want to know?"

She dips her head, her hair curtaining her face. "Yes... No. My head feels screwed up. I don't know what I want."

I take her face in my hands, forcing her gaze upwards. "We'll make sure he pays."

I pull her mouth close to mine and brush my lips over hers. I realise in this moment I will do anything to keep her safe. I will take all her demons and I will fight them. I never want anything bad to touch her again, and as long as there is breath in my body it won't. "Stay in the common room with Valentina."

She swallows hard then nods. I lead her back inside and then walk around to the shed. As I step into the building, I'm greeted by Wrecker hanging from the hook in the ceiling. They've cut his T-shirt down the front, leaving the ragged halves hanging off his arms. His toes barely touch the floor, leaving him swinging from side to side. There is no fear in his eyes as he meets mine. He's made his peace with dying and that pisses me off. I want him to beg. I want him to ask for mercy that I will never deliver. Socket stands in front of him, homicidal rage blazing in his eyes. Blackjack and Terror hold back a little, ready to step in if necessary. It won't be. Socket will have his time and then I will take my turn.

Wrecker meets my gaze, his lips curling up into a snarl. "You burnt my club to the ground."

"You left them to burn."

There's no shame in his eyes, no guilt, either. "You

prefer the captain went down with the ship? Is that what you would have done, Howler?"

I grab him by the throat, my fingers tightening until they whiten under my grip. I get right in his face and hiss, "I would never have left my brothers."

I release him with a shove, disgust crossing my face. Cowardly fucker. "I did what I had to."

Socket steps up, holding a metal pipe in his hand. "Is that what you told yourself when you were raping my fucking daughter?"

I see a flicker of uncertainty cross Wrecker's face. "She ain't your kid."

Socket slams the pipe against his stomach. I see how hard Wrecker works not to cry out. I want to hear him scream in pain, but the fucker has some dignity, it seems. Socket lowers the pipe and with his other hand grabs Wrecker's face. "Oh, she is, and every hurt you put on her I'm going to visit back to you ten-fucking-fold. I'm going to make you cry for mercy. I'm going to push you to the fucking edge and not let you go over it. You're going to die. And I'm the one who's going to decide how that end comes."

Socket steps back and pulls the pipe back like a baseball bat before he slams it into Wrecker's knees. I hear the crunch of bones as the strike is made. This time, the cunt does cry out. He throws his head back and pulls on the chains holding him, making them rattle. Socket doesn't give him a moment of reprieve before he slams them again.

"She's my daughter, you piece of shit!" Socket roars in his face. "You used her like she was nothing."

Years of pent-up rage flow through my brother. All that anger at not being able to claim his daughter, the rage at finding her in the position she was in; it all erupts out of him. He smacks Wrecker in the chest and the abdomen before stepping back. The control in him is clear. This isn't an uncontrolled attack. Socket has planned meticulously what he's going to do to the Jesters' president for maximum suffering.

He moves over to the metal table that contains devices of torture. He drops the pipe onto it and picks up something else. "Did you feel powerful when you were raping my daughter?" Socket demands. When he turns back he is holding a pair of pliers.

Wrecker's tongue dips out and runs across his lips as his eyes dart around. If he's looking for help, he's not going to find it in this room. I want my pound of flesh, too, but I also need to let Socket do his thing.

"I own her. She had debts—"

"She had fucking nothing with you. She married a dickhead, but she wasn't complicit in your fucking sordid business affairs."

I think Socket is going to start removing fingernails from the beds, but instead he forces Wrecker's mouth open. He fights, as I would, too, but Terror and Blackjack step forward to hold him, forcing his jaws apart. Socket reaches inside his mouth with the pliers, and I watch the push and pull as he fights to pull the tooth. Wrecker screams as much as he can with a hand in his mouth. I can hear the crunching of teeth, and, after a minute, Socket steps back holding the tooth with the nose of the pliers. Blood courses down Wrecker's jaw and he gags a little as he tries to spit it from his mouth.

No longer content to just watch, I move over to the table and pick up a blowtorch. I switch it on, watching the blue flame as it dances at the end of the pipe. I like fire. It has the ability to cleanse and destroy. I step up to the prisoner, who eyes me with nervousness. "Didn't know she was Sons property," he says.

"I don't care," I reply. I put the flame to his chest and watch as the skin melts beneath it. His screams are a symphony of joy to me. The smell of it is unpleasant, but I don't stop burning him. When I step back, I see the results of my handiwork. The word rapist is blistered into his skin.

Wrecker is panting now, trying to breathe. We don't give him a moment of reprieve. We go at him hard and heavy. We beat him, we burn him, we pull teeth and fingernails. We employ every method of torture we know. It won't make up for the suffering Pia experienced, but the burn of vengeance is a sweet one for me.

And for Socket. My brother needed this more than I did. Maybe more than Pia did.

He needed to feel useful, protective, like a dad.

I watch as Socket cuts pieces of flesh off Wrecker's arm. He's stopped screaming now and his head hangs limply between his shoulders. I'm not sure if he's even conscious, but for his sake, I hope not.

He is smeared in blood, barely recognisable beneath

the bruising and swelling. I have blood on my own hands, crusted onto my skin. I stare at the man who broke the beautiful woman I've come to love and I realise there is no punishment that fits the crime. No matter what we do to him, it won't undo what was done to Pia.

I step forward and grab Wrecker's hair, forcing his head up. His eyes are glassy, unfocused, as he tries to find me. His Adam's apple bobs spasmodically. I glance at Socket, asking without words if he has had his fill. My brother nods. I turn back to Wrecker. "You deserve so much more than this. We should have raped you, made you feel the same pain you inflicted on Pia. We should have made you beg for us to stop and kept fucking you anyway. We'll never be able to give you the same torment you gave her, but I do take solace from the knowledge your end was messy and painful." Socket hands me a knife and I take it from him. I glance at the blade before I raise my eyes back to Wrecker. "Your club is gone, your world destroyed. She gets to live on."

I drag the blade across his throat, blood spraying over me. I watch his eyes and the panic fill them as he starts to gag and gurgle, choking on his own body fluids. I step back and hand the knife to Blackjack before I move to the sink and start cleaning myself up. I wash the blood off my hands, listening to his choking last breaths. It soothes some of the darkness inside me and makes me feel self-righteous, like I avenged Pia's hurt.

I leave my brothers to clean up and get rid of the body and all the DNA evidence, then head into the shower at the back of the building. It's nothing more than a concrete slab with a drain in the middle. I strip out of my clothes, hanging them on the hook outside the shower. Turning on the water I wait until it's hot before I step under it and then I sluice the blood from my body. My face has the worst of it, and blood matted in my hair takes more than a few moments to wash out.

When I'm done, I use the towel on the rail to dry myself and throw on a spare set of clothes I keep there. I head back into the kill room and snag my kutte off the hook near the door, putting Socket's back in place. I don't pay attention to what they're doing, but my brothers will take a few hours to clean up.

I make my way back into the clubhouse, seeking Pia out, but she's not in the common room. I see Valentina and cross the room towards her. She glances up as I approach and I see the tears standing in her eyes. She blinks them away quickly and forces a smile. "It's done?"

I don't answer her, instead I ask, "Where's Pia?"

"She went to lie down." Valentina grabs my arm as I start to move away. "I know she comes across as strong, but she is falling apart. Don't hurt her."

Her words piss me off, considering how much she and Socket have destroyed Pia. "You really want to go there about me hurting her?"

She shrinks back, but her chin comes up. Prideful to the last. I don't give her a chance to respond. Instead I make my way out of the common room and up the stairs to the bedrooms. I stop outside Pia's room, or the room that has become hers since she's been here. I knock and then enter. She is lying on the bed, her knees drawn up to her chest, the covers pulled up over her.

As I step inside, and shut the door behind me, she sits up. "Is he...?"

I can't read the look in her eyes. There's fear, but there's also something else. Hope. It feels good knowing that we have removed the source of her nightmares. She never has to fear Wrecker coming for her again. I protected her; I kept her safe from him.

I move to the bed and she shifts so I can sit on the edge of the mattress. "You don't have to worry about that piece of shit." Despite the harshness of my words, I reach out and tuck her hair behind her ear in a gentle gesture. Fuck, I love this woman. I will do anything to keep her safe. Nothing will touch her as long as I have breath in my body.

She wraps her arms around my neck and hugs me as if her life depends on it. As she sobs, I pull her close, not wanting to let her go. She is the breath in my lungs; she is the blood in my veins. She is the electrical pulse that keeps my heart beating. She is mine, and I am hers.

I kiss her face, tasting the salt of her tears and vow in this moment that nothing will ever make her cry again. She will only know good things. She will only know happiness.

And she will never have to hear the names Wrecker or the Road Jesters again.

Her mouth finds mine and she kisses me. My hands roam up under her top, to the silky skin of her back. I need her, in ways I have never needed anybody. She completes me, makes me feel human. I've never had this connection with any woman before, and I want to keep hold of it desperately.

I go back onto the mattress, bringing her down on top of me. She straddles my hips, her hands cupping my face as she devours my mouth. This kiss is claiming, and I'm not sure who is claiming who. "I love you," she gasps between kisses. "Thank you."

I peer up at her, my heart pounding in my chest. I hold the whole world in my arms right now, and I don't know how that makes me feel other than inadequate. "You're mine. I want everyone to know it."

There is barely a hair's width of space between our mouths, and her warm breath washes over me. "What do you mean?"

"I want to claim you."

"You want to make me your old lady?" She pulls back and I can see the surprise in her face.

"I don't need to do it officially—you are mine—but it will give you better protection if everyone knows it."

She closes her eyes for a moment, as if trying to calibrate her thoughts. I use my thumb to swipe at the tear that's rolling down her cheek. "Jake."

"Say you'll be mine."

She opens her eyes, which are full of tears. "Yes, yes." She laughs as she says it. My heart swells. "I'll be yours."

I pull her back down to me and I kiss her as if she is my reason for breathing, because she is.

CHAPTER 19
PIA

I wake with a warm body at my back. Jake's beard tickles the back of my neck where he's burrowed in. His arms are wrapped around me tightly, as if even in sleep he didn't want to let me go. I feel safe with him, in a way I never have. There aren't many men who would kill to keep their woman safe, and while I know I should be disturbed by that, I'm not. It makes me feel loved and I like it.

For a while I just lie in his arms, soaking up his touch like a giant sponge. I never expected to find someone who would want me after what I have been through. Maybe one day I will be able to tell him the sordid story of what happened to me, but I don't think he will care if I never am able to talk about it.

He starts to stir behind me, and as he wakes he nuzzles in deeper into my neck. "Morning," he says in that gravelly voice of his. It makes between my legs flutter in a way I never thought would happen again. I want to be with him, but I think that will take time. I have to heal, both emotionally and physically. He doesn't seem to be in a rush, though, and his patience gives me the confidence to find my voice again.

"Hey," I say softly. I tilt my neck as he starts to kiss down the column of my throat. The gentleness of his actions is so at odds with the gruff exterior he gives out. Don't get me wrong; I know Jake is dangerous. He kidnapped Max and held him in the shed. I don't even want to know what he did to Wrecker. The less I know the better. But I also watched him burn down the Jesters' clubhouse. He's not a man who fears repercussions. He will go to the edge for those he cares about and that means something.

"What are you thinking about?" he asks.

"How much you've done for me. I can never repay that."

"Don't want payment, babe. Would be fucking offended if you tried."

His hand runs over my stomach, making the muscles beneath it quiver. His touch has the power to ignite me. "You protected me in ways nobody else has," I insist, then change the subject.

"I talked to Gavin. My dad." I laugh a little. "It feels strange to call him that. I never imagined I would meet my father. He was lost to me for so long."

"Ain't going to tell you what to feel, or what to do, but I will say this. When Socket faced that fucker who hurt you, he didn't hold back."

I don't know how to feel about that. I don't say

anything, letting my thoughts drift. Jake doesn't push me for anything. He just keeps his hand on my belly, as if he can cage me against him. "I don't know what to do with that information, Jake."

"Don't expect you to do anything with it. Just telling you what happened. He made sure Wrecker got what he fucking deserved. He did that for you."

I swallow hard, trying to dislodge the lump growing in my throat. "He abandoned me for two decades of my life. I don't know him."

"Folk don't get second chances a lot in life," Jake says. "Seems like you've got one with your father."

He's right. There were times growing up when I would have given my left arm to be able to meet my dad. I used to go to sleep and pray that he would turn up the next morning to take me out somewhere. I think about all those times I lay in bed, wanting him, yearning for the parent I lost out on. "There's a lot of hurt."

"Yeah, babe, I can imagine there is. Socket will be waiting when you're ready."

"My mum loves him."

His fingers still on my stomach before he continues drawing circles again. "Yeah, she does."

"Isn't this every kid's dream? For their parents to get back together again?" I exhale on a heavy breath. "Is it stupid to want it, considering I'm a grown-up?"

"Doesn't matter how old you get. They are still your parents."

I turn around, needing to face him. His hand comes

back to rest on my hip as soon as I'm settled in front of him. My eyes scan his face before I speak. "You said you wanted to claim me last night. I know what it means to be an old lady. I was with the Jesters long enough to glean some of the lifestyle."

A snarl plays across his lips. "We ain't nothing like those fucking deadbeats."

I rub a soothing hand over his chest. "I know you're not. Believe me, I saw the worst they had to offer. All I've seen since I've been with the Sons is good men. I know exactly what I've gotten myself into here. I just meant I know it's a big deal."

This seems to take some of the anger out of him. "Yeah, it is. Makes you as close as a wife to me in the eyes of the club. Means no one will touch you. Everyone will take care of you, but it does come with responsibilities, too. Expectations. As old lady to the president there will be things I need you to do."

"Whatever you need," I tell him, meaning every word of it.

He leans forward slightly, closing the gap between us, and presses his lips to mine. The kiss is hot and heavy. I take his hand and place it on my breast. He pulls back a little. "We don't have to. "

I meet his eyes. "I want to feel your hands on me."

He kneads my breast through the thin material of his T-shirt I slipped on for bed. His eyes remain locked on mine, seeking any discomfort, but all I feel is trust.

"I want to undress you."

I lift my arms and let him pull the T-shirt over my head, leaving my tits bared to him. He drops his gaze to my nipples and heat flares through me at the hungry look in his eyes. Then he latches his mouth onto my tit.

He sucks the nipple, his tongue laving around the bud. My back arches of its own accord. It's as if there is a direct link between my nipple and my pussy. Tingles race through my pelvis as he continues to work me over.

I thread my fingers through his hair, which is longer on the top and shaved short on the sides. I can hear my breath catching as he starts to work me up to a frenzy. I keep my thoughts locked only on him, not allowing anything else to break through. I don't want anyone else in this space while we are connecting like this. "I'm going to touch your pussy," he says. I know it's his way of telling me what to expect next, but the filthy words make my pussy clench with anticipation.

"Yes."

As soon as the word spills from my mouth, he cups me between my legs, even as his mouth remains locked on my breast. He rubs me through my underwear, moving his thumb over my clit until I'm writhing. I put all my trust in this man. I give myself over to him completely, knowing he will not hurt me. Knowing all he seeks is my pleasure. It lets me get out of my head long enough to enjoy what's happening to me.

I press my hand against his cock, feeling him semi-hard beneath his boxer shorts. His own breath catches this time, his teeth scraping across my breast, and it spurs me on to continue stroking him. Feeling brave, I slide my hand down the waistband of his underwear and run my fingers over his silky shaft. I run my fingers around his cock and I twist as I pull up, my movements are slow but purposeful. I want him to enjoy this as much as I am. I want to show him I'm not broken and that I can do these things.

I keep working him as he keeps playing with my tits. His hand moves to my waistband and I will myself not to freak out as he slides down towards my bare pussy. As his fingers trail through my folds, I'm so focused on him and what he's doing that I don't give it a second thought. "I'm going to put my fingers inside you," he says in a soft voice. I nod, wanting that, too. "Need the words, babe."

"Yes, please do that."

He pushes two fingers inside me even as he continues to play with my clit with his thumb. I can't stop from moaning as he slowly pistons in and out of me. My pussy feels electrified, contracting around his fingers as I build closer to my orgasm. I let go of everything, of the past, of what happened to me, of the trauma suffered, and I focus only on him. The way he loves me, the way he takes care of me, the way he protects me. It's enough to push me over the edge. I go over with a strangled moan that seems to erupt from my belly. Barely a moment later he grunts and I feel his cum spray over my hand as he releases his own orgasm.

He pulls his fingers from me and sucks them into his mouth, tasting me, claiming me. My mouth dries. He kisses me, and I can taste myself on his lips. It shouldn't be hot, but it is.

We should shower, but instead I tuck myself against his chest and I let myself drift off, knowing I'm safe and secure in the arms of my man.

EPILOGUE
HOWLER

THREE MONTHS LATER...

"You sure you want to do this?"

I glance up from where I'm leaning against the wall, my boot pressed against the brick. Pia is a few feet away, talking to Valentina. Even though I know the threat has passed, I don't let Pia out of my sight. If I can't be with her, then there's a prospect on her at all times. I plan to keep my promise that nothing will ever touch her again.

Valentina shakes her head. "I know you think I need protecting, but I don't. I want to make this work. I want a chance with your father."

"I know but running off to get married like two wayward teens—"

Valentina takes her daughter's face in her hands. "Life is short. I already spent decades away from the man. I won't spend years more. I love Gavin. I always have. In twenty-odd years that hasn't changed. I want him to be my husband and I want desperately to be his wife. I don't need a showy affair, Pia. I just need him and you."

My woman mulls this over for a moment before she huffs out a breath. "If that's what you want who am I to stand in the way?"

Valentina smiles and that smile grows wider as Socket approaches. He steps up to Valentina, his hand going to cup her cheek. I can see how much my brother loves her. It's written in every line of his face. It's the same way I look at his daughter.

I watch Pia carefully, noting the uncertainty as she waits. Then her father's gaze locks on her. He doesn't move, though I can see he's itching to go to her.

"Darlin'," he says in a soft voice. I've noticed he's only gentle like that with his girls.

"Mum says you are eloping."

"Mean a lot to us if you are there too."

Pia glances over her shoulder at me and I shift my shoulders. If she wants to go, I'll not stop her. But she knows the drill. Ain't being left behind.

She turns back to her parents, glancing between them. "Okay. When are we leaving?"

"In about an hour," Socket says. He reaches out and skims his fingers over his daughter's face. "I know you don't believe this, but I do love you, kid. I always have."

She pulls her bottom lip between her teeth, something she does when she's trying not to cry. I resist the urge to punch the fucker standing in front of me who brought these tears on.

"I know." The words are spoken in barely more than a whisper, but they carry as if she shouted them. "I'll go and get ready."

She walks off as my gaze meets Socket's for a moment. I see the pain there, the anguish that he can't rebuild the bridge he destroyed with his daughter as fast as he wants to. She'll come around. She does every day little by little, but this isn't a quick fix. There is no magic wand that can be waved to magically make the past disappear. He and Valentina made their choices, and now they have to live with the consequences.

I push off the wall and Socket says my name.

I glance back at him.

"Wasn't always the biggest supporter of this shit between you and Pia," he admits. I snort. No shit. "But I can see you have her best interest at heart. I feel fucking better knowing you're taking care of her, Prez."

"I fucking love her," I say before I turn and follow after Pia as she walks from the garden into the common room. I catch up with her as she steps into the corridor, then snag her wrist and twist her, pushing her against the wall behind her. There's no fear in her eyes as I bracket her with one hand pressed into the wall just above her head and one to the side of her hip. Fuck, she's beautiful. I want to claim her lips, devour her. I want to show her all the ways I can make her happy. I push my hips against her as I take her mouth. She tastes like fucking heaven.

I skim along her tongue, before I suck it into my mouth. I love kissing her. I love touching her, being with her. She gives my life fucking meaning that it never had before.

I pull back, my mouth scant inches from hers, our breaths mingling as we breathe heavily. The trust in her eyes when she looks at me makes me feel fucking whole.

"You don't have to go," I tell her. I don't care if that pisses Socket off, but I won't force Pia to do shit she doesn't want to.

"They're my parents. They're getting married. I can't miss that." She ducks her head and shakes it a little, as if trying to clear the thoughts from her brain. "My entire life I've dreamed of this moment. I hoped my father would come back and we could be a family." Her eyes find mine and I see the anguish in them. "So why am I not happy?"

"Because you're hurting, babe."

Her nose wrinkles.

"I want to just let it go, move on, but I can't—not yet."

"Then don't. No one is saying you have to do this on their timeline. You're pissed at them, be pissed at them. You want to make it work, make it fucking work. You don't owe anyone shit."

"The stupid thing is I am happy that they're sorting their crap out. I'm thrilled my mum found someone who loves her. Thrilled I have my family." She buries her head in my chest, her fingers gripping the edges of my kutte. "Why am I like this?"

I take her shoulders and carefully push her back off me. "Whatever you're feeling, just own it. No one expects you to just forgive and forget in an instant. This shit takes time."

She raises her head and gives me a smile that melts my fucking heart. "I think the universe was smiling down on me when I met you."

"You do?" I ask, pushing her hair off her face.

"I do. I don't deserve you, but I'm not giving you up, either."

"I wouldn't let you anyway."

I watch as she pulls her bottom lip between her teeth. Those plump lips are ripe for the fucking taking. "We have an hour before we have to leave for the registry office." There's a hint of playfulness in her tone. I'm fucking glad she suggested it because I want her so badly right now.

"And what do you want to do with that hour?" I ask.

She leans up onto her toes so that her mouth is inches from my ear and says, "I want you to fuck me."

I pull back slightly. We've done other shit, but I've never been inside her. We tried a few weeks back and it threw her into a panic attack. I haven't attempted since.

"Babe, no."

She licks her lips and I can see how nervous, but how determined she is. "I want this."

I brush my fingers through my hair, pushing it off my forehead. "Pia…"

Reaching up, she places a finger on my lips. "I'm tired of waiting. I'm ready."

She grabs my hand and tugs me towards the stairs. Fuck, is this a good idea? I don't fucking know, but my woman is fucking determined as she pulls me up the stairs and down the landing towards our room.

As soon as the door is shut behind me, I turn to her. "You're sure?"

She nods.

"Any time you want to stop—"

"I know," she says. "I trust you. I know you won't hurt me, Jake."

Fuck. That she is putting herself in my hands like this makes me want to fucking roar. The trust she has is out of this world, and I swear to fuck I will never shake that faith she has in me.

I push her up against the wall and attack her mouth. Desperate neediness overtakes me. I want her and I've wanted her from the moment I laid eyes on her. The thought of being inside her shakes me to my core.

She kisses me like I'm her reason for breathing, and I like that. Because she's mine. She'll always be mine. I'll fight to keep her safe, to defend her. I'll fucking give my life if it keeps her protected.

My tongue slides into her mouth, duelling with hers, and my hands slide up under her top until I reach the band of her bra. With two fingers I unhook it, and I break apart from her kiss just long enough to strip her out of it and her T-shirt, then our mouths fuse together once more. I bend over, latching around her nipple, sucking on the bud until it's hard. She cradles my head, her fingers threading through my hair in a way that makes me want to fist my fingers in hers. The last few months have been hard for her. It took her a while before she was able to stand me touching her pussy without throwing her into some kind of fucking flashback. Every day I cursed that we didn't make Wrecker and his cunt brothers suffer more. I should have taken them to the brink of death just to bring them back and do it again.

For the past month, she's been seeing a therapist who specialises in this kind of trauma. It hasn't worked miracles, but it has given Pia strategies to deal with her past, to tackle her panic attacks and keep her grounded. It helped us to get past the hurdle that upset her the most—her inability to be intimate with me.

I didn't need a fucking therapist to tell me how to help Pia. Instinctively I knew what she needed. She needed to know I was safe. That I'd never hurt her like those fuckers did.

So over the months I've built trust between us. I show her I will never fucking take something she hasn't freely given to me. I do that every day and I'll probably have to do it every day in our future, but I'll give her anything to help her heal.

I knew when she was ready she'd let me know. I didn't expect it to be now, though I should have. She's become more bold, more confident in the past few weeks. Knowing she's in control calms those old fears and I think —I hope—she knows I'm not going to force shit on her ever.

The dirty talk is fucking new though and I fucking like it.

I'm hard as fuck in my jeans as she pushes her own down her legs. I see a flicker of uncertainty, but it passes before I can call her out on it.

"Any time you need to stop," I say.

"Make me come," is her response.

I don't need another invitation. I don't bother undressing, I just drop to my knees and grasp the back of her legs as I pull her cunt against my lips. She tastes fucking divine and I swirl my tongue in her wetness, lapping up everything she's giving me. I love this woman with everything I have.

I keep swirling and spearing my tongue into her cunt, each flick over that bundle of nerves making her thighs tremble. I fucking love that. I love bringing her pleasure.

She tips her head back against the wall, her eyes shutting as her palm presses against the paintwork. Honestly, she's never looked more fucking beautiful, standing here naked, ready for me.

I lick and suck at her clit, making sure to pay attention to her breathing. It tells me when I'm in the right spot. Her pants are heavy as I continue to eat her out, her juices spreading over my beard.

"I'm going to—" She breaks off into thick pants as her orgasm rolls over her.

She fists her tits as she breathes through it, but I don't give her a chance to come down. I stand, unzipping my jeans and pushing both them and my boxers down my thighs. I give my dick a couple of tugs, but it's not necessary. I'm already hard as a rock.

"You want me to fuck you?" I ask, giving her a chance to back out if she needs it.

Her molten eyes meet mine even as she continues to knead her tits.

"Yes, Jake, I want you to fuck me."

I lift one of her legs, giving me a better view of her pretty pussy. Then I use my other hand to guide my cock into her.

I feed it inside her inch by inch, watching her eyes carefully as I do. There's no sign she's in distress or about to spiral into a panic attack, so I push deeper until I'm buried to the root. She reaches down for my free hand, the one not holding her thigh up, and interlaces her fingers with mine. That connection is more than physical. I can't exist without this woman, and I hope she feels the same.

I raise our joined hands over her head as I start to move inside her.

My strokes are slow, steady, and deep. She groans every time I push into her, her little pants making my cock even harder.

"Love you." I tell her something she already fucking knows, but in this moment it feels important to reiterate it. I've waited so long for this moment and it's better than I could have imagined. Her cunt contracts around me as I continue to pump into her. I kiss her face and neck as I fuck her.

"Love you too," she says back.

I slam into her, making her try to squeeze her thighs together, but I'm holding her leg so she can't. "Fuck, Jake…"

I keep my eyes locked on hers as I fuck her into another orgasm. Her cunt contracts around my dick, squeezing it so hard I come a moment later, spilling my cum inside her. She's on birth control—neither one of us ready for a kid right now—but I love seeing my spunk dripping out of her. Fuck if it doesn't make me want to roar my fucking triumph. I place my hand on her belly, knowing she'll look fucking magnificent growing my kid inside her.

She dips her head, leaning against my shoulder. "Fuck," she mutters. "That was... *fuck...*"

I laugh as I pull out of her. She cups between her legs, trying not to make a mess. I tuck myself back into my jeans, but don't fasten them as I move to the bathroom and grab some tissues and wet a cloth under the tap.

When I come back into the room, I hand her the cloth, which she uses to wipe between her legs.

"You want to shower before we have to leave?"

She nods. "I need to change into something more wedding appropriate, too."

"Babe, you know your dad is going in his kutte. I've known the man years and I've never seen him in a fucking suit once. Not even at weddings, funerals, or fucking christenings."

"That doesn't mean I can't dress up," she says.

I run my hand over her back as she bends to pick up her tee off the floor where it somehow ended up.

"Love you in a fucking dress. Love you in jeans. Love you in nothing."

She gives me a side glance. "You're biased."

Yeah, I fucking am. She leans up and kisses me. "Keep me company?"

I follow her into the bathroom. We shower together,

washing each other. When we're done, I step out and grab a towel, wrapping it around my hips.

In the bedroom, I dry and dress while she does her usual routine of picking clothes. Once I'm dressed, I pull on my kutte.

"Meet you in the common room," I tell her. She'll be ages getting ready. Love her, but I don't have the patience to wait while she does her hair and makeup.

"Okay," she says.

I walk out of the room, feeling that unease I always feel when I'm not with her, but she's safe in the clubhouse. Nothing can fucking touch her here. She has the protection of every member of this club, and not just because she's Socket's kid, but because she's my old lady.

I created a fucking fortress to keep my family safe, and she's part of that family now.

I head down to the common room and see Blackjack sitting at the bar. My VP has been fucking quiet the past few weeks, which isn't outside the realm of normal for him, but I can tell something is bothering him.

I sink down next to him, patting his shoulder.

"Socket and Valentina are getting married," he says.

"Yeah."

"Pia pissed?"

"Ain't sure what she is, to be honest." Blackjack peers out over the back of the bar, not seeing anything, and I say, "Ain't big on heart to fucking hearts, but you need anything brother—"

"Just tired. Been hitting the tables a lot lately."

Cards. My brother is a fucking whiz at blackjack,

which is how he got his road name. I've seen him take money from big players like it's fucking candy. The admission doesn't explain the fucking morose mood he's been in for weeks.

"You lose?"

He snorts. "Are you fucking joking? No, I didn't lose."

"Blackjack." At the sound of Terror's voice we both turn on our stools. My brother is standing behind us, a small petite redhead with him. I've never seen this bitch before in my life, but Blackjack comes off his stool, making it fall back.

"Told you if I saw you again, I'd fucking put a bullet in you. It wasn't a joke."

She nibbles on her bottom lip. "I know," she says. "I wouldn't be here, except I need your help."

He closes the space between them and grabs her arm, pulling her away from us. I watch the unfolding chaos between them and the tension, readying myself in case I need to step in. He is rough as fuck, but no one moves to intervene. This shit is between them.

"You got a fucking death wish?" he hisses.

Her reply is softer, barely carrying across the room, but I hear it. "I need your help."

"No."

"Please, Matt."

The use of his real name tells me everything I need to know. They're close, but he's never mentioned or brought this woman to the clubhouse. I've never fucking laid eyes on her before this moment.

"Ain't fucking falling for that routine again, bitch," he

snarls, dragging her towards the door. She fights against him, but he has brawn on his side. My brother is built like a tank. "I learnt my fucking lesson."

I wonder what she did to him. I've never seen my VP so angry.

"Let fucking go of me!" She tries to twist out of his hold, but he doesn't release her. "If I could take that back I would."

"You can't."

Her eyes dart around the room, as if realising she's not in friendly territory, but I see the fear there. It's deep-seated. "He's going to kill me, Matt."

"I don't care."

"You should," she says quietly. "Because I'm pregnant… and it's yours."

My eyes slide towards Blackjack, who is staring at her as if she just told him she's fucking Satan.

"The fuck are you talking about?"

"I'm pregnant," she repeats.

Blackjack grinds his teeth together and then he hauls her out of the room.

I glance at Terror who shifts his shoulders.

"Fuck."

GET A FREE BOOK AND EXCLUSIVE CONTENT

Dear Reader,

Thank you so much for taking the time to read my book. One of my favourite parts of writing is connecting with you. From time to time, I send newsletters with the inside scoop on new releases, special offers and other bits of news relating to my books.

When you sign up, you'll get a free book.

Find out more here:

www.jessicaamesauthor.com/newsletter

Jessica x

ENJOYED THIS BOOK?

Reviews are a vital component in any authors arsenal. It enables us to gain more recognition by bringing the books to the attention of other readers.

If you've enjoyed this book, I would be grateful if you could spend five minutes leaving a review on the book's store page. You can jump right to the page by clicking below:
https://books2read.com/Howler

ALSO BY JESSICA AMES

Have you read them all?

UNTAMED SONS MC SERIES

Infatuation

Ravage

Nox

Daimon

Until Amy (Until Series and Sons Crossover)

Levi

Titch

Fury

Bailey

Stoker

Cage

FRASER CRIME SYNDICATE

Fractured Vows

The Ties that Bind

A Forbidden Love

UNTAMED SONS MC MANCHESTER SERIES

Howler

Blackjack

Terror

IN THE ROYAL BASTARDS SERIES

Into the Flames

Out of the Fire

Into the Dark

IN THE LOST SAXONS SERIES

Snared Rider

Safe Rider

Secret Rider

Claimed Rider (A Lost Saxons Short Story)

Renewed Rider

Forbidden Rider

Christmas Rider (A Lost Saxons Short Story)

Flawed Rider

Fallen Rider

STANDALONE BOOKS

Match Me Perfect

Stranded Hearts

ABOUT THE AUTHOR

Jessica Ames lives in a small market town in the Midlands, England. She lives with her dog and when she's not writing, she's playing with crochet hooks.

For more updates join her readers group on Facebook:
www.facebook.com/groups/JessicaAmesClubhouse

Subscribe to her newsletter:
www.jessicaamesauthor.com

- facebook.com/JessicaAmesAuthor
- twitter.com/JessicaAmesAuth
- instagram.com/jessicaamesauthor
- goodreads.com/JessicaAmesAuthor
- bookbub.com/profile/jessica-ames